I0557045

Powhantuwa's River

First Book
in
The Riverbooks Series

Yvonne Dorsey

COPYRIGHT

Powhantuwa's River
copyright 2014 - Yvonne Dorsey

Written and Printed in
the United States of America

Previously published
by same name and author

ISBN: 978-069-2202-395

Powhantuwa's River

No part of this book may be reproduced by any means, without written permission from the author, Yvonne Dorsey, or a legally appointed representative of Yvonne Dorsey.

The above rule includes, but is not limited to, electronic, mechanical, magnetic, photographic, photocopy, or by any storage system.

This book is fiction. All characters are the sole creations of the author. Resemblances to any person, living or dead, or any rites and traditions are coincidental.

The author accepts no liability for anyone who reads this book and applies any of the scenarios to his/her life.

The author accepts no liability for any information about geography, rites, or traditions of the First American Nations.

All situations presented in this book are written with regard for the hardships the ancients endured; for loves they lost and found, for prayers they prayed to a deity they served.

In the imagination of the author, it is about their reverence for their Good Earth and, about their ordinary, or not so ordinary, everyday life.

It is about people, young and old, good, and bad, who lived those lives.

CREDITS

Story   Yvonne Dorsey

Photography

Choptank River,   Yvonne Dorsey
Maryland

High Bridge, New Jersey   Rose Dorsey Ranauro

Cover Model:

Native American Woman   Kimberly Helen Pickell

Model's Photographers   Rose Dorsey Ranauro
                                   Corey Matthew Ranauro

Sketch on Back Cover
Feathered Cross   Kimberly Helen Pickell

Cover Design   Keith David Ketterer

ACKNOWLEDGEMENTS

I thank my special readers for their insightful
comments and suggestions.
No person listed here received compensation for
reading and commenting on this book.

Keith Ketterer	Susan Hayes
Corey Ranauro	Eleanor Irons
John Perry	Mary Kay Mitchell
Rose Ranauro	Marjorie Goble
Marilyn Stowell	Buck Boccansuso
Wallace Dorsey Sr.	Jim Fealey
Marie Rush Beck	Anne Walters
Patricia Rush Beck	Kinberly Pickell
	Katherine Bagin Theleman

INTRODUCING
THE RIVERBOOKS SERIES

This First Book: "**Powhantuwa's River**" is a fictional ancestral account for the characters in the second book:

Second Book: "**Run to My River**" by same author.

Both books are precursors to a final story in the second section of **Run to My River**, "The Haunting of Shannon Fitzpatrick," which was set in motion centuries before Shannon was born, on a river she loved.

The Girl in the Coal Camp House" by same author: two stories in one book: "The Haunting of Shannon Fitzpatrick," and "The Haunting of Kally Glenn."

It is a story of two women, grandmother, and granddaughter, born fifty plus years apart, being haunted by the same little girl with big sad eyes, standing at a window pleading for help. This confuses Shannon Fitzpatrick. While researching family notes and stories to uncover the mystery, she uncovers a family member's secret.

Read
Run to My River
and
The Girl in the Coal Camp House

PREFACE

The heart of Little Fox was pounding; her bare feet bleeding and burning. Though blinding tears were covering her face, she continued to run from her village as fast as she could, toward the deepest part of the forest.

Every step was agony as sharp blades of grass along her path whipped her legs.

She clutched her one-week-old baby daughter close to her own bosom, praying she was not smothering her.

Haunted by memories of the violence she just witnessed, Little Fox fought the urge to scream; crying, "Please help me, Great Spirit. Please save my baby." Hoping to keep her baby quiet, she put a finger in its mouth to suck. The gentle tugging of the baby was reassuring as she ran, but suddenly it stopped sucking.

Little Fox was sure she had smothered her but was afraid to stop to examine her. She continued running, held it close to her chest and decided that even if her baby died, it would still be a more merciful death than the vicious savagery that had just silenced her entire tribe.

CHAPTER		PAGE

CHAPTER ONE
Little Fox, Mother Love

One hour prior to Little Fox's escape, the small Powhantuwa Village was humming with the sound of morning. The religious leader had finished his morning prayers to the Great Spirit; and the villagers were going about the activities of the day. Children were laughing as they played games of tag. Young lovers were seductively touching each other's bodies while doing their chores. Young mothers were hushing their babies with the nourishment of mother's milk.

Older women were pounding grain for the mid-day meal. Men were busy hunting, fishing, and trapping. Returning anglers were displaying their catch from the river. The revered great-grandmothers of the tribe sat weaving.

It was a warm morning. The flowing river provided a cool breeze. Remaining yellow of spring bushes provided a golden perimeter for the eating compound. Sweet aroma of ashes from the early morning fire lent an air of home to the peaceful village. The first crops of summer berries were ripe for picking. Blue Cloud, chief of the tribe, sat with the elders, smoking his pipe by the dwindling embers.

Suddenly, shrieking sounds, coming from the west, staggered and stunned the unsuspecting tribe. Blue Cloud looked up from his smoking pipe to see wild barbaric riders attacking the villagers. The attackers seemed to know he was the chief of the tribe, for they grabbed him, brutally beat him, and tied him to a tree, forcing him to witness the annihilation of his people. Blue Clouds mate, Satuwa, screamed, calling him by name. She tried to run to him. One attacker, realizing she was the mate of the chief, grabbed her by her flowing hair. He swung her around and threw her to the ground. She screamed as she fell. Another attacker joined him. They kicked her repeatedly. She moaned and passed out. Her son-in-law, Young Wolf, tried to rescue her. One attacker at once beheaded him.

Satuwa was bleeding from her mouth and other orifices of her body, but the barbarians did not want to end her misery too soon. They dragged her to the tree where they tied Blue Cloud. She awoke to see his face. The savages tied her to the feet of Blue Cloud, forcing him to witness her agony and death.

Blue Cloud cried to her, "Satuwa, I will soon be with you. Go peacefully to the Great Spirit." She looked at her life companion and tried to speak. No words surfaced. Blue Cloud moaned as Satuwa took her last breath. The barbarians continued their attack. They rode their horses over scurrying members of the peaceful tribe; even the children; trampling them to death.

When the assailants finished their brutal foray, all members of the village lay dead, including the friends of Little Fox, who had returned from berry picking. The attackers slightly stabbed the chief in his side, wanting the flowing blood to give him a slow death.

Little Fox and her friends had been only a short distance from the camp, picking berries for the noon meal. They had picked an abundance and were returning to camp when the baby of Little Fox cried. Little Fox insisted the others go on without her. She felt she was close enough to the village, to travel alone. Her friends returned to the village.

Little Fox sat and removed her sandals, to rest her feet while she nursed her baby. As she was preparing to tuck her baby back in the pouch, she heard horrifying sounds coming from the direction of the village. She rose on her knees, peered through the brush, and saw the attackers tossing sticks of fire into the tents to chase out the inhabitants.

The horrible sight of wild men swinging weapons, severing heads from the bodies of her tribal family, horrified and frightened Little Fox. Seeing the decapitation of Young Wolf, the father of her baby, she screamed but held her hand over her mouth to muffle her voice. Her heart was pounding. She could feel the beat, beat, beat, in her temples.

Her first impulse was to run to her people, but her mother's instinct was to save her offspring. She did not take the time to gather the baby's pouch, nor to put on her sandals. She crouched and quickly backed her body into the woods. She watched and listened intently for any invader who might chase her; pausing only long enough to re-wrap the baby tighter in its blanket. She was still fearing a savage might chase her. She ran for as long as she could.

Only when she thought she might be out of danger did Little Fox stop briefly to rest. She cried with relief at the sight of her peacefully sleeping baby. She wanted to let out thankful praises to the Great Spirit for sparing their lives. She resisted, for fear of being heard by the murderers who had just dehumanized her village.

Little Fox thanked the Great Spirit for helping her escape, for she knew that her baby daughter had saved them both when she cried to nurse.

The young mother trembled and sobbed at the remembrance of the horrible sights and sounds of the brutal scene. Although she was thankful that she and her baby escaped the inhumane violence, she felt guilty they were the only one who escaped.

Hoping the baby, with a full belly, would sleep and be quiet, Little Fox nursed it again, wrapped it in its blanket, and then resumed her journey toward the southern portion of the river. By then she was almost certain no one was following her, but the horrendous sight of the massacre plagued her as she ran. She did not look back. Remembering the cries of her people, she almost screamed aloud.

Knowing she needed to get as far away as possible, on and on she fled, alternating between walking and running. She resisted crying, so she would not exhaust her precious energy. The pain in her bare feet was becoming more intense with each step. Knowing several large peaceful tribes who lived along the river, Little Fox hoped someone would rescue her. She especially wished for asylum with the tribe of the Choptank.

The Choptank Chief, Red Wolf, once visited the Powhantuwa Village. Little Fox felt a kindred spirit toward him. She hoped he was still their chief; and that his people would allow her to raise her daughter among them in their village. If not, then possibly they would take her daughter to rear as one of their own. She was hoping they would allow her to leave peacefully. Her concern for her daughter's safety and survival was more important to her than her own young life.

Needing to nourish her own body to care for her baby, Little Fox munched on berries from her pouch, plus some she found along the way. She hurriedly dug roots to eat. When she felt she put enough distance behind them she dared to stop and rest again. Hoping she was out of harm's way, but still fearing for the life of her child, she rested only a brief time. She was at the mercy of nature, and all animals sharing that nature.

Fighting hysteria, she sobbed for Young Wolf. The memories haunting her were almost unbearable. She felt faint, but she

4

knew she had to stay alert if she wanted to save her baby. She scurried for the rest of the day, only stopping occasionally at a stream to refresh herself and the baby.

The Great Spirit was surely aiding the young woman, for miraculously, no animals threatened her. Though it was nearing darkness, she felt she was traveling in the correct direction, toward the Choptank Village. Her heart was pounding as if it would explode in pain. Blood dripped from her nose. She stumbled and staggered through the high brush. Although no one attacked her, she still feared someone might be chasing her. She stumbled against small trees.

Finally, she felt the coolness of sand under the grass. She saw no inhabitants; the villagers were obviously preparing for sleep, but she felt certain she had reached sanctuary. Nearly crawling, she reached the riverbank. Seeing the river, she cried aloud, ran to it, and stepped into its water. The water burned her swollen, bruised feet and stung her thorn scratched skin, but was comforting to her tortured soul.

She tried to splash herself without getting the baby wet. Realizing her weakened state, and that she might pass out, she moved away from the water, eased her body down and fell on the sandy ground, still holding her baby. She passed out. The little one was content, secure in the arms of her sleeping mother.

After about an hour, Little Fox awoke. Her body trembled from the damp sand and her exhausting journey. Fearing she had dangerously exposed her baby daughter to the cool mist too long; she arose and moved away from the water's edge. She was sure she had arrived at the village of the Choptank. She prayed she had made the right decision to run to them.

The cool night mist of the river was refreshing, but Little Fox knew she needed to keep her baby warm. Looking around, she saw a large rock.

In the moonlight, it resembled a giant mother bird with high wings. The backside of it was close to the bank. Hoping it will give them some protection from the night wind, she struggled to get behind it. Having done so, she fell to the ground, desperately needing sleep, but wanting to care for her child.

She took off her own garment and wrapped it snugly around her already bundled baby to provide extra protection and warmth. She cuddled the baby close to her own naked body and laid her on her own belly to keep her off the cold sandy ground. Then, she put her to breast to nurse. The baby suckled, cooing sweetly.

As Little Fox watched her tiny daughter nurse, she sobbed until she was sick. She was in shock from her devastating ordeal and bleeding from her recent birth. She tried to keep her tears, and the blood dripping from her nose, from falling on the baby's face. Crying for her mate, Young Wolf, she cradled her daughter.

The little Powhantuwa baby continued to make sweet cooing and sucking noises as she partook of nourishment from her mother.

Little Fox said a weak prayer of thanks to the Great Spirit. Being sure she had reached a haven, she fell asleep. The caw of night birds awakened her. She cuddled her infant and listened to the sounds of nature.

The night was becoming day. Shadows of trees and rocks were coming into view. The rush of flowing water beating against the huge rocks was a soothing sound.

The clouds seemed to move to the clangor's rhythm. The tranquil harmony of nature and the cooing of her child caused Little Fox to cry again. The young woman, barely mature, with only a few days to learn to be a mother, studied her child's face as if trying to place it in memory. She held its tiny hand in her own, caressing and kissing each little finger. The baby opened her eyes and looked at her mother. Little Fox put her face to the head of her tiny daughter and cried. She pulled the coverings securely around the infant to create a shelter. She held the bundle in her arms to keep it off the cold sand and then placed the baby's face close to her own body. She had done all she could to provide and protect her baby. She knew the Great Spirit was in charge.

Looking up at the sky, Little Fox smiled as if she recognized the person standing over her. She tried to raise one arm to touch the vision but was too weak to do so. She imagined she saw moving clouds gently enveloping her own mother, Satuwa. The scene before her was one of peace. Memories of her life were flowing in front of her. She remembered when she became a woman and then of her mating with her sweetheart, Young Wolf.

Cuddling her baby closer, Little Fox smiled as she remembered the pain and joy of giving birth. The baby continued to coo. She raised her little hand and touched her mother's neck. Little Fox kissed the little hand and gently tucked it back in the blanket.

The gentle touch of mother and babe, which should be one of bonding, only brought sobs. She tried to hum a soothing lullaby but could only manage sad, soft moaning.

Little Fox had mixed emotions as she watched several images swirling around her. She saw her tribe dancing around in a giant circle, laughing as they twirled. She heard drumbeats. Many,

many colors were coming in and out of view. Again, she saw her tribe dancing. She heard more drumbeats.

Music was in the air. The spirit of Young Wolf extended his hand toward her. Again, she tried to raise her own hand to his. Finally, Young Wolf spoke, "Little Fox, take my hand. Do not be afraid. I will take you to the Great Spirit." Little Fox longed for Young Wolf, but her heart was aching; she cried when she realized her earthly time with her daughter was nearing the end. In her delirium, she wondered if she would take her baby with her, across the river. The little logic she still had dictated that she should protect her child and give it a chance to live.

As the last act of an eternal mother's love, Little Fox, again put her baby to nurse; to sustain her for as long as possible, praying that someone would find her.

More clouds replaced the faces in her vision. The sounds became serene. She made one last imploring plea to the Great Spirit for the safety of her baby daughter and closed her eyes in eternal sleep. Only then could she take hold of Young Wolf's outstretched hand and join the family in their dance. For a moment, she looked back and smiled. She saw a young couple standing nearby. She motioned to them, but they did not acknowledge her.

Little Fox knew her little Powhantuwa baby was in safe hands. She whispered to her child, "I will always be with you." Her gentle spirit joined the soul of Young Wolf.

They went dancing to the Great Spirit.

CHAPTER TWO
The Prayer Rock, Haven for Little Fox

A long the shore of the Choptank River sat a pile of rocks that were so close, they seemed as one giant rock. The largest of the piled-up rocks loomed over the rest and resembled a giant bird's wing preparing to soar to the sky.

The tribe referred to the collection as the 'Rock' or the 'Prayer Rock,' sometimes, 'The Praying Rock.' They believed the Great Spirit designed the rock as their sanctuary. They held many ceremonies, funerals, and other celebrations around it; prayed many prayers near it and rubbed many tears on its rough surface.

Lovers made their marks on it to declare their union. Women sometimes sat by it to pray for their men who were rowing canoes out to catch fish. Children played around it.

Families buried the bones of their deceased loved ones on the higher ground nearby. Summer, Autumn, Winter, Spring, the rock was a place of solace and strength to the peaceful people who occupied the land of the Choptank River.

Laughter was a common sound. It was their spiritual place.

The Choptank River flowed from an enormous body of water from the west.* The fearful inhabitants called it, "The Big Water." They told many tales of the powers of the measureless water. Most of the inhabitants believed the Big Water was the home of the Good Spirits, and they did not dare to go into it. Others just viewed it as too deep and dangerous.

When the Choptank chief, Red Wolf, died, his eldest son, Moon Dancer became the chief of his tribe. Moon Dancer always loved a young girl of the tribe, Running Doe. On the day, he became chief; he selected her to be his mate. Orphaned Running Doe, raised by her older sister, Hoquia, knew she needed to produce a male child, a future chief for the tribe, but she had not concerned herself of that fact. She reasoned that she and Moon Dancer were young; a male child would surely bless them by his birth.

Running Doe and Moon Dancer spent many late nights and early mornings by the giant rock. Whether they were holding hands, making love, or praying, the 'Rock' was an important part of their life. The death of a young woman, by that special place provided a daughter for them.

* Chesapeake Bay

CHAPTER THREE
Answered Prayer from the Rock

Early in the morning, after the death of Little Fox, Chief Moon Dancer went to the riverside to meditate before the tribe gathered for morning prayers. As he sat in meditation, he thought he heard a soft sigh. He stood and followed the sounds coming from the back of the giant rock.

A naked dead young woman was clutching her newborn baby, wrapped in her discarded clothing. She had protected her daughter by sacrificing her own life. He sadly picked up the tiny baby and asked, "Who are you my little one? Am I to name you Little Rock?"

Trying to avoid viewing the young woman's nakedness, Moon Dancer took the baby away from the lifeless body and walked around to the front side of the rock. A surprised Running Doe joined him.

Moon Dancer said nothing. He pointed back to the dead body.

Running Doe ran behind the rock. She instantly covered the body of the young mother with leaves and branches; crying as she worked. She took off her own shawl and held it open. Moon Dancer laid the baby in it. He pulled the young mother's garment from the baby and laid it over the body.

Tears filled the eyes of Running Doe as she re-wrapped the baby. She sighed, "The mother looks so young. What happened to her?" The thought of a young mother fleeing with such a newborn saddened her.

Moon Dancer and Running Doe had a few minutes before the gathering of the tribe. They sat in front of the Prayer Rock to await the assembly. When Running Doe was tending to the baby's cleansing, they saw that it was a girl. The members soon gathered. It surprised them to see a baby in Running Doe's arms for they did not know she was with child.

Moon Dancer instructed them to stay on the front side of the Prayer Rock. He then discussed the sadness with them; declared that if no one claimed the child, she was his daughter. Moon Dancer ordered a new mother to share her breast milk with the newborn.

Traditionally, when a member died, the tribe gathered to pray for its happy journey home to the Great Spirit. They build a high bed, placed the body on straw and dried leaves. They set the bed on fire to purify the body. The spirit of the deceased then elevated to the Great Spirit.

According to their custom, the women prepared the body of Little Fox; the men built the tall funeral fire bed. The entire tribe chanted long and loud to the Great Spirit for her soul. They celebrated her life and said many prayers for her as if they knew her. Finally, they prayed for her blessed journey across the river to her eternal home.

Moon Dancer secretly told Running Doe that he recognized the mother's garment as one of the peaceful Powhantuwa Tribe. He had gone with his father on trips to their village as a boy and remembered the visits of the Powhantuwa Chief, Blue Cloud, to their village.

Although the Powhantuwa Tribe was peaceful, it had not joined the 'protective alliance' with the other tribes of the Eastern Shore. Moon Dancer said he would try to return the child to them. Later, when they were alone, Running Doe argued against Moon Dancer's decision. She asked, "Why do you think the young mother fled with her child, Moon Dancer? Did you not see her scratched and bruised body? She was running for a long time. Do you not think you are making a mistake, taking the baby back to the same people she was fleeing?"

Moon Dancer made no comment. He had already thought about keeping the baby as his own and ignoring his duties. No one outside his tribe would know. However, he knew his moral responsibility was to find the family of the tiny baby peacefully sleeping in the arms of his mate.

Running Doe held the baby's face close to her own. She was secretly hoping the Powhantuwa Tribe did not want the baby returned to them.

In the three years, Running Doe had been the mate of Moon Dancer, she had not borne a child for him. Suddenly, she had the joyous fulfillment of motherhood. As she held her newly gained baby daughter, thoughts of another child, even a son, were far in the recesses of her mind.

For Moon Dancer, hopes of a future leader of the tribe; evidence of his own virality and manhood were all-consuming. Sleep did not come easily for either of them that night.

Early the next day, being accompanied by a group of braves, Moon Dancer left to travel north to the Powhantuwa Village. He agreed to leave the baby with Running Doe until he was sure it would be safe with its own people. As he traveled, he stopped at other villages to greet the tribes who shared the peninsula.

Whenever there was a meeting of the tribes, the visiting party carried a Staff of Peace, usually a string of white feathers tied on a tall pole. Chief Moon Dancer always followed that protocol.

Several tribes of the Eastern Shore had entered an agreement; they would live and hunt only on their own territory. These area tribes had also agreed to patrol the borders to protect the entire Eastern Shore. Though they had been patrolling, somehow the clever Shanaquoix, in the dark of night, sneaked onto the shore.

On the way to the Powhantuwa Village, they stopped at the village of the Metapoke. Their leader, Chief Dark Eagle, recounted the raid on the Powhantuwa Village: "Several of our braves, hunting on our side of the Powhantuwa Village, heard screams. When they reached the village and saw the slaughter, they surprised the brutes of the Shanaquoix tribe and killed all of them. They found only one living person, Chief Blue Cloud. The savages had tied him to a tree and left him to die a slow death. They must have killed his mate in front of him, for she lay dead, clinging to his feet."

Moon Dancer asked, "Was the Great Spirit kind to let him die soon after?" Dark Cloud answered, "No, but he was barely alive." He then led Moon Dancer to a tent. The 'Healing Elder,' the medicine man, pulled back the cover to allow entry.

A dazed and injured Chief Blue Cloud lay on a blanket, staring blankly into space. Dark Eagle said, "He has been like this since my braves found him." Moon Dancer knelt in front of Blue Cloud. He said to the older chief, "There is one alive. A baby sleeps in my village. A young woman brought her to us. She died, but we will care for the baby until you are well. Then you can decide what to do for her. She is yours."

Blue Cloud's expression never changed. Moon Dancer was hopeful the older chief understood his message; that he would remember the baby was in complete safety until he could care for her. Dark Eagle assured Moon Dancer that he would continue to remind Chief Blue Cloud of the presence of a remaining member of his tribe.

During their meal, the two chiefs discussed the Shanaquoix; a cruel aggressive tribe who lived on the Western Shore: The Shanaquoix chief wanted to own the fertile Eastern Shore.

The attackers had made large canoes to cross the Big Water to conduct that mission.

The chiefs reasoned that the plan of the Shanaquoix was to hide out in the newly unoccupied Powhantuwa Village and then to sneak more and more of their braves past the border patrol and once they were many in number on the conquered territory, they planned to hit all the peaceful villages simultaneously, and then take over the entire Eastern Shore.

The brazen attack on the Powhantuwa Village convinced the two leaders they needed a stronger plan of defense if they were to be successful in protecting their land. Chief Dark Eagle was already preparing to send Braves to each tribe when Moon Dancer arrived in his village. He planned to discuss more aggressive defense with all the tribes of the eastern shore.

The two tribal leaders discussed the remaining uncommitted Eastern Shore Tribes who needed to join them to form an organized, aggressive Protective Alliance. Before Moon Dancer left the Metapoke, he arranged a return trip; a meeting the next day to discuss the alliance with the other tribes of the peninsula. On his way home, he stopped at each small village to report the invasion and to encourage the other tribes to join the discussion.

When Moon Dancer returned to his own village, he summoned his tribe to gather and related the horror of the Powhantuwa

15

Village to them. It saddened Running Doe to hear of the slaughter. She joined the assembly as they prayed for the healing of Blue Cloud. However, she feared that if he ever recovered, he would come after the baby, the only remaining member of his tribe.

Moon Dancer said he made a promise to surrender the baby to Blue Cloud once he could care for it. He would keep his word.

As Moon Dancer's words sunk into the mind of Running Doe, her heart was sinking deep within her soul. She was content, but covetous with 'her' baby daughter and always sat close to the nursing mother during each feeding. Though she was glad the baby could share the nourishing mother's milk, she was envious of the lactating mother and always took the baby away as soon as the nursing was complete.

Running Doe hoped the Powhantuwa Tribe had sent the young mother away for some shameful reason, and the young mother wanted sanctuary with the Choptank Tribe. This thought gave her credibility as the recipient of the child.

With the account of a living chief, Running Doe faced the reality of losing the baby. Before going to sleep, she discussed the situation with Moon Dancer. She began with, "He will have to find a mate who will care for the baby." An exhausted Moon Dancer answered, "Yes, I know."

Running Doe continued her strategy as she was settling in their bed, "She is still at the breast, you know." Moon Dancer's only response was a nod of his head. As they cradled the baby between them, Running Doe knew all conversations about Chief Blue Cloud and the baby were over.

Moon Dancer made a promise. That was that.

The next day Moon Dancer, again being accompanied by a group of braves, went to the meeting of the alliance. Running Doe spent the day holding and rocking the baby, only releasing her occasionally to the nursing mother. She secretly wished Moon Dancer would come home and tell her the Powhantuwa chief had died. Then she would have full rights to the baby.

Immediately feeling ashamed, she prayed, "Great Spirit, forgive me for my wickedness. Please do not harm Moon Dancer for my sins. I know the child should be with her people, even if it is only a tribe of one. Please make me strong to accept what is right."

When Moon Dancer returned, he called the members to gather by the Prayer Rock. When all were assembled, he announced, "Hear me, what I say." He continued, "The strong and cruel Shanaquoix, who live on the other side of the Big Water,* want to kill all tribes so they can have our land.

"We have declared a larger and stronger alliance with all the tribes on our side of the *Big Water. Together, we will be a stronger nation. We will be on constant patrol. In the morning light, I will choose braves from our tribe to be a part of the new patrol. Each chosen Brave will take a turn at guarding our shorelines. The northern tribes will guard the narrow way to the other shore. I will soon travel to make talk with the southern tribes."

Moon Dancer continued, "We will not try to go to the Shanaquoix Village to attack them, but we will prepare for battle. I am hoping the Shanaquoix will leave us in peace. I have spoken again to Chief Blue Cloud. He could not speak, but I feel certain his spirit understands what I say to him, that the baby girl is healthy. I will name her Powhantuwa, so someone will remain a member of his tribe."

With those words, Moon Dancer took the baby from the arms of Running Doe.

Running Doe breathed deeply as the baby, high in the air, began to cry. Moon Dancer declared, "Today, I call you Powhantuwa, for you are the survivor of your tribe." The baby cried. Everyone cheered, danced, and prayed for the crying baby.

Running Doe also prayed for the baby but stood in wait for Moon Dancer to return it to her waiting arms. When he finally did, she held it close to her own tear-streaked face. Moon Dancer knew what was in her heart. Losing her new daughter would cause her severe emotional pain, but he had made a vow and intended to keep it. Duty was paramount.

For several days and nights, Running Doe and Moon Dancer seldom spoke of Blue Cloud. The thought of him coming to claim his one remaining tribal member was a constant dread.

Running Doe reasoned that the chief was dead. She felt sure the Metapoke had no interest in her daughter. Moon Dancer, though he would not admit it, was bonding with the baby.

CHAPTER FOUR
The Dreaded Visitor

One warm spring morning, Running Doe, with ten-month-old Powhantuwa in her arms, was walking back to the village after their morning cleansing in the river's edge. Suddenly, people were scurrying for shelter. Fearing the worst, she tightened her hold on her child and ran to the forest. Powhantuwa cried because Running Doe held her so close.

Running Doe, trying to calm her daughter and keep her quiet, put her face to the child's face and slowed her run to a walk. She felt she had gone far enough to for the moment, but if there were enemies in their camp, they would soon roam the woods. She continued to hold Powhantuwa near her and crawled under some overhanging brush. She pulled branches around them to create a hiding place, then rocked the toddler to sleep. Soon, she heard several voices. With trembling hands, Running Doe pulled back a tiny branch. To her delight, she saw several young Choptank braves. One called out, "To you in hiding; we have visitors from the Metapoke."

Although the Metapoke were friends, their name struck a sick chord in Running Doe's heart. She remembered them as the host and caregiver of Chief Blue Cloud and feared they were there to take Powhantuwa.

When she reached the encampment, she was unprepared to see a handsome, gray-haired, Chief Blue Cloud sitting with Moon Dancer and the Metapoke chief, Dark Eagle. Blue Cloud looked strong and healthy. The past ten months had treated him well. He appeared strong and healthy. Stifling threatening sobs, she walked toward the trio with Powhantuwa in her arms. Moon

Dancer nodded to Blue Cloud and then looked at Powhantuwa. Blue Cloud stood and held out his arms. A reluctant Running Doe laid the toddler in his arms.

Powhantuwa cried and reached back for her mother.

Running Doe knew she was losing her daughter. She looked up, bowed to the three chiefs, then went to her tent. She could not stop the flood of tears covering her cheeks. Hearing Powhantuwa crying even louder, she buried her face in the blankets to drown her own sobs.

After a few minutes, the mother of Moon Dancer, Little Bird, carried Powhantuwa into the tent and handed her to Running Doe. The baby was still crying. Running Doe guessed her job was to quiet the baby, so the chiefs could talk and eat. Little Bird said, "Chief says to feed her, and then come to council." Running Doe questioned, "Council?" Little Bird answered as she walked out of the tent, "Yes. I will wait for you. We will walk together."

As Running Doe fed Powhantuwa, she felt as if she were just a caregiver. Little Bird heard her grumble, "I am only a nurse for his child. That is all."

Little Bird wondered if Running Doe meant Moon Dancer or Blue Cloud. She felt sorry for her daughter-in-law, but her son was chief. His word was law. She tried to console Running Doe. She said, "the Great Spirit knows your heart. He knows the heart of Moon Dancer. He will give you a child soon. You will see. Please do not be angry with Moon Dancer. He is a good man and chief, but he is also a friend to the Powhantuwa chief. He must keep his word." Running Doe nodded. She knew the words of Little Bird were true. She told her mother-in-law, "I will not grieve Moon Dancer. I will make him proud."

Little Bird picked up the Powhantuwa baby and gave her a toy to occupy her during the council. She set her in the pouch on the back of Running Doe and said, "Let us go." The two women, Mother and Grandmother, began the walk they had dreaded for many months.

The sky was a vibrant blue. Farther down the river, gulls were hungrily but patiently watching and waiting for the opportunity to catch their lunch. Children were running and playing on the shore. Mothers were rocking babies. A young boy was strumming gently on a small drum.

Members were sitting on the beach and riverbank. Running Doe could not appreciate the beauty of the day. Her only thought was one of anger toward the visitors. When she and Little Bird approached the assembly, they saw the handsome Chief Blue Cloud standing with the two other chiefs. Blue Cloud looked at them and smiled. Running Doe smiled meekly back at him. She immediately resented him. He was in her village for one purpose, to take away her child.

Little Bird, although saddened by the same thoughts as Powhantuwa, felt compassion for the older chief. She remembered his visits to their village in years past. Chief Blue Cloud watched her take the baby from the pouch and hold her until Running Doe removed the pouch from her own back. He watched her hand the baby to Running Doe. He smiled again. Little Bird smiled back at him as she joined the older women. Running Doe sat next to Moon Dancer, with Powhantuwa on her lap. Moon Dancer stood and raised his hand high to silence the crowd. He nodded to Chief Blue Cloud and then sat on the ground next to Running Doe.

Chief Blue Cloud arose. He looked up at the sky and then at the crowd. He spoke, "Many moons have come and gone since I have last visited your village. I remember some of you. It was a happier time. Now, much has happened at the hands of our enemy, the Shanaquoix. Much sadness has come. My people have suffered, but they now live in peace with the Great Spirit. For me, good sleep would not come for many moons. When I closed my eyes, I saw the faces of my people. I could still hear their screams as the brutal Shanaquoix cut their heads from their bodies." I was haunted by the vision of the slaughter."

As the chief continued to describe his grief, the faces of the tribal members displayed their extreme compassion for him. He took a deep breath and said, "I remember the blood draining from the wounds in their sides. Each morning, I look at the sky and ask the Great Spirit to forgive me. I built a village too close to the *Big Water. I am to blame for settling my people there. We were a small tribe."

Blue Cloud looked over the assembly and sadly said, "I should have joined a larger tribe for our protection. I was too proud. We were not a part of the alliance, for we could not send our few men out of our village as a patrol."

Running Doe could not concentrate on Blue Cloud's words of pain nor sympathize with him. She had her own. She sat quietly, clinging to the squirming toddler. She was not prepared for his continuing plea. Blue Cloud lowered his head for a moment, and then continued, "Now, I grieve for my sins. Now, I have no people to lead. I am not fit to lead. I have a heavy heart." He sighed as he continued, "The faces of my people, the memory of their screams and the blood of my mate thrown on my face are too sad for me to bear. They are always with me. I was in a sad dream for many, many moons, but I could hear voices.

The Great Spirit sent spirits to comfort and care for me. The kindness of the Metapoke and the Choptank people sustained me. You have all helped me keep my face to the sky. As I rested in the blanket given by the Metapoke and drank broth made by the women of the tribe, I remembered hearing the words of the chiefs. I prayed, in thanks, for your kindness. For many moons. I prayed for guidance from the Great Spirit. Now, I need to care for the little one you have named Powhantuwa. She is my granddaughter."

Running Doe took a deep gasping breath and exclaimed, "Granddaughter?" Her stomach sickened. She was speechless, for she knew she would surely lose her daughter. Immediately, she hated the Metapoke for bringing Blue Cloud to her village.

The sun behind Blue Cloud was at its brightest, creating a glow. As Running Doe stared at his silhouette, she heard him say, "The spirits saved her for me. My daughter, Little Fox, was safely away from our village picking berries during the attack. By the hands of the Great Spirit, she had her baby daughter with her. My daughter died to save her child. The baby's father, Young Wolf, died trying to save my mate. I am Powhantuwa's only family."

The memory of the slaying interrupted Blue Cloud's speech. He paused for a moment and then said, "The Metapoke have treated me good. They have brought me to get my child. Chief Dark Eagle has offered me to live with them, so I can live safely with my child as she grows."

Blue Cloud said the dreaded words. Running Doe tried to suppress her grief. She angrily thought, "His child? She is not his child. She is mine." Her stomach became even tighter. She was nauseous. Her dread had become a reality. She knew she had lost Powhantuwa. Crying softly, she held her even tighter. Moon Dancer and Running Doe held tightly to each other's hands, trying to hide their parental fears as Blue Cloud continued, "The mate of Dark Eagle has offered to care for my granddaughter, but now I see the care you have given her. "You have loved her as your own. I cannot take her from you, but it causes me pain to leave her. I have spoken to your chief and the chief of the Metapoke. Now, I ask you to accept me as a member of your tribe and allow me to be a part of your village. I am too old to start a new village, but I am not too old to work for yours. If you allow us to stay with you, Powhantuwa would know me as her grandfather, and I could tell her about her people. She can still be with you if you want her. Now I sit and wait for your answer." With that last statement, the humbled chief sat in the sand. Blue Cloud's display of emotion saddened the tribe.

Relieved and excited by his request, Moon Dancer, and Running Doe stood at once. Running Doe, holding little Powhantuwa in her arms, walked to the chief. She knelt and gently placed the baby girl in his arms. Blue Cloud accepted his granddaughter. He held her close to his face and gave in to the combined emotions of grief and joy. Streams of tears fell on his face. The crowd cheered. After many months of his emotional prison, they gave him the gift of a family reunion. The Powhantuwa baby looked at the chief with questioning eyes, as if she knew he was a special person in her life. She did not cry.

Acknowledging the gesture of their leader as a "Yes" vote, members stood. The entire tribe was circling the chief of the Powhantuwa in acceptance of him as their new tribal member. They danced and chanted to the Great Spirit in thanks and celebration. Moon Dancer pulled Running Doe close to his side. They looked down at the older man sitting in the Prayer's middle Circle. Blue Cloud looked up to them. He held Powhantuwa so tightly that Running Doe wanted to take her from his arms. She resisted the temptation and smiled instead. He managed to weak smile back at her. Running Doe felt ashamed for her selfish hopes he might be dead. She looked down at him as he held the toddler. Tears were running down his cheek. Little Powhantuwa put her lips to her grandfather's cheek to lick his salty tears. She appeared to be kissing him, causing more tears for Blue Cloud.

When he could no longer hold the squirming child, Blue Cloud smiled and held her out to Running Doe, who gladly accepted the little one. She held Powhantuwa's face close to her own. She knew that for Blue Cloud's continued healing: he needed to be with his only family member, his grandchild. She was glad he was there in the Choptank Village and thankful that she was still holding her precious gift from the prayer rock, her daughter, the little Powhantuwa Princess. Blue Cloud's behavior would normally be disgraceful for the chief of a tribe, but he was no longer a chief. He was a grieving man with a loss too much to bear. The chief dismissed the tribe. Running Doe took Powhantuwa to her nap. Little Bird stayed behind with the older women to serve refreshments to the three chiefs.

Days went by. Seasons changed and changed again. Months turned into years. Powhantuwa fulfilled the joy of motherhood for Running Doe. The little girl was now a happy little five-year-old, playing on the beach and fields, doing small chores, playing with her friends, and spending a lot of time with her grandfather, Blue Cloud, and her grandmother, Little Bird.

The entire tribe who called the adopted child "The Powhantuwa Baby" referred to her as "Powhantuwa;" a beloved reminder of the history of the near-extinct Powhantuwa Tribe. The tribal members had called Blue Cloud, "The Powhantuwan." Later, they called him "Blue Cloud." They could not use his title as they had a chief.

Blue Cloud and Little Bird formed a close friendship. It was comforting for them to be with a member of their own generation. He loved the name, Little Bird, as it reminded him of the name of his daughter, Little Fox. His friendship pleased Little Bird.

Early one cool autumn evening Blue Cloud sat by the river. His mind was on the memory of his dead mate, Satuwa. He smiled at the memory of her carrying their newborn grandchild from the tent of their daughter, Little Fox. As he reminisced, he recalled another time that filled his heart with joy. In his daydream state, he recalled: His daughter, Little Fox, was a two-year-old toddler.

One day, when he was meeting with leaders of the tribe, she came running to him and jumped up on his lap. He scolded her for coming to the meeting, but Little Fox just smiled, caressed his cheek, and lay her head on his chest. The tribal leaders tried not to show any emotion but were smiling at the control the little girl had over their chief. The toddler slept while he conducted tribal business.

As other memories came to mind, Blue Cloud smiled. He remembered Little Fox and Young Wolf dancing after their Mating Ceremony, and Young Wolf dancing and chanting to the Great Spirit when he realized he was to become a father. Sweet memories changed to extreme sadness as Blue Cloud remembered the morning of the massacre. Little Fox, carrying her newborn baby, came to the morning fire. Blue Cloud held out his arms. Little Fox handed him the child. How thrilled he was to hold his first-born grandchild.
Little Fox said, "We will pick berries." Blue Cloud, fearing the berry bushes might scratch the baby, tried to persuade his daughter to leave her with Satuwa. Little Fox declined, thinking the baby might grow hungry. Blue Cloud was grateful the Great Spirit guided Little Fox to the Choptank Tribe. He said a silent prayer of blessing. As tears threatened him, Little Bird, knowing when to join him and when to stay away, came and sat beside him.

CHAPTER FIVE
Remembering the Waters

Powhantuwa was growing increasingly into the likeness of her biological mother. She was beautiful. She loved the river. One day, when she was seven years old, Moon Dancer watched her and Running Doe as they played in the water.

Being a mother thrilled Running Doe. She seemed to have forgotten her responsibility to produce a son. Though Moon Dancer loved Powhantuwa, he still needed a male heir to, someday, become chief of the tribe. As he sat, he remembered a happier time when he went to sleep each night with Running Doe's face before him. That memory was fading day by day.

He remembered that he wanted to become the mate of the orphaned, Running Doe. His father, Chief Red Wolf, forbade him to touch her until she was a full woman. Running Doe was equally eager to become his mate, not because he was a future chief, but because she loved him deep in her soul.

One day as they were scratching their marks on the Prayer Rock, pledging their eternal togetherness, Running Doe teased Moon Dancer, saying, "I will give you many sons to go hunting with you." She often teased him with her youthful body.

Moon Dancer became a young chief when his father died. When Running Doe was available for mating, she celebrated her womanhood by ceremonially running with her friends. She bathed in the river; her friends adorned her with flowers. Finally, the young couple stood in a 'Mating Flower Circle' and become one. She finally joined him in his tent. Except for hunting and fishing expeditions, they were constant companions, Even though the tribes viewed a female, even the mate of a chief, as nothing more than a vessel and servant, Moon Dancer treated Running Doe as an equal. They were soul mates.

Another memory came to Moon Dancer as mother and daughter played,: even before the death of his father. He had said, "Running Doe. I have a place I want to show you." Running Doe never questioned him. He said the round trip was a long journey. When Hoquia, Running Doe's sister and guardian forbade her to travel unescorted, Moon Dancer agreed to take her with them.

The next morning, they prepared blanket rolls for their journey, then rode their horses southeast, away from the Northwestern *Big Water. For protection, they took along a few young men.

After they had traveled for a while, Moon Dancer suggested they stop and eat their meal. Hoquia worried that they had traveled too far from the village. Running Doe was not concerned. She was happy just to be with Moon Dancer. Suddenly, she halted her horse, and took a long, gasping breath.

The sight of the endless waters in front of her was more wonderful than she could ever have imagined. Hoquia was equally captivated. The young escorts jumped from their horses and ran to the edge of the water. Moon Dancer halted them. He had been excitedly waiting for the group's reaction to his surprise. He watched as their faces glowed with excitement at the magnificence of the water before them.

The sky and the water had no division; they seemed as one. Moon Dancer announced, "You cannot see any land beyond it. It is the *Great Waters."

*Atlantic Ocean

The sisters stared in amazement. Moon Dancer gave the young men permission to stand near and touch the flow and ebb of the water but forbade them to go into the deeper part.

When the rushing incoming and ebbing water did not harm the young escort, the girls jumped from their horses, removed their sandals, and ran toward the ocean. The breeze from the turbulent water whipped at their hair. They barely felt the broken shells piercing their feet.

The tremendous wall of foam, rising high over the surface, violently ascending, and descending, becoming waves that pushed the water toward them was frightening, yet exhilarating. They halted, fearing to step any closer.

The sand moved quickly through their toes, then back to its home, the ocean.

The sight before them was more than wonderful. For their entire life, the two girls had only seen a flowing river.

Hoquia feared they had reached the end of their world because she could see no land beyond the ocean. She wanted to leave, but Running Doe was in love with the ocean and with Moon Dancer. She would have stayed there forever if he suggested.

Moon Dancer took Running Doe's hands and playfully pulled her to the edge of the water. After a few minutes, the sand moving under her feet was becoming sensual. She laughed nervously as she tried to play in the water. She said, "Look, Hoquia." Pointing to the white caps of the ocean, she added, "See how the water jumps up to reach the clouds. Moon Dancer said, "Chief Red Wolf showed me this Water when I was young. He believed the Great Waters was a sacred place and the jumping water was the Good Spirits from the Clouds, bathing.

He said no people should go into their water or make their mark on the sacred ground. I came here for my Vision Quest.*

Moon Dancer smiled proudly and said, "I played in their waters. The waters never harmed me. I told no one. My father would not have approved."

Running Doe laughed and said, "I will tell no one." Hoquia agreed. Running Doe said, "Moon Dancer, I will have my ceremony soon. After I run with my friends to celebrate my coming of age, I can come to you in your tent. Hoquia has already spoken to Chief Red Wolf."

Running Doe's words electrified Moon Dancer's senses. She knew what she was doing. She wanted him. Resuming her suggestion, she said, "If this is a sacred place, we can pray to the Great Spirit to bless us here. I can run here, with Hoquia, on this sand. We can make our own 'Flower Mating Circle' and become mated right here with the jumping spirits. We can live by this wonderful water. It will surely bless us, and we will have many sons."

Hoquia knew Running Doe wanted Moon Dancer all to herself, away from the tribe, and wanted to share him with no one, but she was still shocked by her sister's boldness. Moon Dancer, though he loved Running Doe's suggestion, did not comment. The thought of her in his tent clouded his mind.

After their meal, and one last look at the magnificent waters, they began their ride back to the village. Moon Dancer could see Running Doe was enjoying the journey. He could also see she was pleased with her ability to raise such diverse emotions for her traveling companions.

(*Male solitary proving time)

Powhantuwa's River

As they traveled, Moon Dancer was aware that someone was watching them through the high bushes. It had not concerned him. The local inhabitants, who knew him as a leader of a friendly northern tribe, had purposely kept their distance.

Gleeful screams brought Moon Dancer out of his reverie and brought him back to watching his family play in the water. Powhantuwa called out for him to join them. He waved to her and smiled. Running Doe also tried to persuade him to join them. He rose and turned to walk away. He looked back to Running Doe, feeling sad that he had lost the enthusiastic love he once had for her. That love was changing to resentment. He wanted to love her as he once did, but she had no time or regard for him.

Powhantuwa, again, pleaded for her father to come into the water. He waved to her but continued walking away.

Running Doe, not even noticing the sad look on the face of Moon Dancer, playfully grabbed Powhantuwa and twirled her around. Powhantuwa wanted to run after her father, to bring him back to join in their play. She loved her parents, but even at the early age of seven, she was aware of the tension between them.

Later in the day, Powhantuwa, carrying a plate of food, hurriedly walked to the fire area. She wanted to sit next to Moon Dancer for their evening meal. He smiled at her as she tried to settle down beside him. She tripped, spilled her bowl of food, and cried. Moon Dancer asked her, "Why do you cry, Powhantuwa? Go to the cook and get another bowl of food."

Powhantuwa went away crying. When she did not return, Moon Dancer asked of Running Doe, "Why has Powhantuwa not returned to eat? Why did she cry? I did not scold her."

Running Doe said Powhantuwa was probably with her friends. She did not convince Moon Dancer. He left the fire area and went to look for her. He found her on the riverbank, talking to the wind. Instantly, he wondered if an evil spirit was trying to take control of her soul. He called out to her. She turned and ran to him. Clinging to him, she said, "Moon Dancer, please do not be angry with me."

Moon Dancer laughed and said, "It was a little bowl of food, Powhantuwa. Why do you cry over a little bowl of food?"

Powhantuwa answered, "I see you so angry with me and Running Doe many times when we are playing. I want you to be with us, but you do not wish to. I am afraid you are sorry you took me from the rock. If the rock gave you a boy, would you be happier?"

Moon Dancer was ashamed of displaying his anger toward Running Doe in the presence of their daughter. He said, "Look at me. See my smile. I have a love for you. I love you as my daughter. You have brought Running Doe and me much joy. I am never angry with you. You please me as my child. Believe me when I say this. I have other thoughts on my mind and sometimes I look angry. I am chief. I need to care for all our people. I have many problems to solve."

He reached out for her hand and asked, "Now, could we go to our meal?"

Powhantuwa smiled at her father, dried her eyes, took hold of his hand, and happily skipped back to camp.

CHAPTER SIX
Betrayal

Another year passed without a pregnancy for Running Doe. She and Moon Dancer were becoming more distant, spending less and less time together.

Powhantuwa's grandparents spent most of their days together, playing with Powhantuwa, or just watching the flowing river. Many tribal members thought it improper; that their advanced ages dictate they mourn their mates until their own deaths. Moon Dancer disagreed, and as their leader, gave his blessings on any relationship they desired.

Though Powhantuwa often played with her friends, she spent most of her time with her grandparents. Running Doe was glad, for her own playfulness was waning.

One day, while Powhantuwa and her grandparents were enjoying a day by the river, Running Doe took time alone. The stress between her and Moon Dancer was increasing because she was barren. Sometimes, she feared he would cast her aside, keep Powhantuwa for his own, and find another mate. These were her thoughts as she walked along the river. Reaching a pile of rocks, she walked around them and up the bank to the grassy field that led to the forest.

Disregarding the danger of walking in the forest alone, she headed in that direction. As she approached the edge of the forest, she saw a herd of deer farther along the riverbank. She stopped and observed them, thinking,

"How beautiful they were. Never mind the old Buck sends the little ones and his doe out in front of him to check for danger."

She started to make a loud noise to scare them off but was in too sad a mood to be playful. Instead, she, being careful to mark her path, walked into the forest.

After walking a short distance into the forest, a loud moan startled her. The first impulse was to run to help whoever was in trouble but decided against it. Afraid of an enemy attack, she hid under thick bushes.

The moans got louder. She smiled, realizing it was simply the sound of two lovers enjoying each other's bodies." Wishing she could avoid interrupting them, she stayed hidden. She could not block the sound of their personal time. It would have been embarrassing if the lovers felt the wife of their chief was spying on them.

A familiar loud cry from the male struck a horrifying chord in the heart of Running Doe. The sounds of sexual release echoed in her head. She cried aloud, "Moon Dancer, oh no, not Moon Dancer." Clasping her hands over her mouth to keep from screaming, she cried, "Moon Dancer, how could you? How could you? You are my lover. You are my lover."

Running Doe's sadness turned to contemptible anger. Gritting her teeth, she grabbed a rock. She wanted to scream at the other woman, to bash the blood from her head and then pound the body of Moon Dancer deep into the ground. She wanted to scream filthy words of extreme revulsion at the cheating pair. She was one ball of loathing. Fear quickly replaced the anger that arose in her. She put down the rock and sank to the ground, quietly sobbing.

While the lovers were together, Running Doe continued to clasp both her hands tightly over her mouth to stifle her cries. She prayed to the Great Spirit for endurance in her silent grief. She prayed the couple would soon leave. She wanted to run from the sounds, but the wrath of Moon Dancer, if he heard her, kept her from taking that risk. She reasoned he was secretly planning to have her put to death and take his lover as his new mate. She cried inwardly, "What should I do? What should I do?" Her head was bursting. The sad thought that Moon Dancer's intention was for his lover to become pregnant, was distorting her logic. Her heart was throbbing with the pain of losing his love, but uppermost in her mind was the pain of losing her child.

Regardless of her situation, and the thoughts that haunted her, Running Doe had to endure the post-sexual conversation of her mate and the other woman. She knew her silence was vital to her own survival. She dropped her head into her lap and remained in that position until she heard the familiar sounds of Moon Dancer's loud snore resonating from his 'conquest bed.'

Soon, the young girl appeared from the bushes and walked toward the more isolated banks of the river. Running Doe recognized her as Singing Bird, a girl who had recently become a woman eligible for mating. It was all coming together. Moon Dancer was more than anxious that he had no son who would become a future chief. The evidence was apparent. He was taking matters in his own hands.

Negative thoughts were distorting Running Doe's logic. She quietly came out of hiding. As she walked, she thought if Singing Bird became pregnant; she would become the mate of Moon Dancer. It would not matter to him if she produced a girl child; the proof she could bear children would be enough. A boy child would soon follow.

Running Doe's mind was whirling as she walked. Fearing for her own survival, she followed Singing Bird; certain she would choose a secluded cove of the river to cleanse her body of her newly exposed womanhood and to wash her garment. She quietly approached the cove and watched as Singing Bird removed her garment and stepped into the shallow area of the river.

Running Doe had witnessed the birth of Singing Bird; had shared her life. She was sick at the thought of what she had to do, but she could not allow her to bear the child of Moon Dancer. The sounds of the forest and the splashing water in the cove provided a muffler. She quietly inched closer to the naked girl. As she did, she picked up a heavy tree limb and yielded a solid blow to the girl's head.

Singing Bird made a small sound as she fell face down, into the water. She cried as she pushed the lifeless body of the beautiful young girl into the flowing water. She wrapped the girl's garment around a heavy rock, walked out as far into the river as she dared and, struggling to stand firm in the rushing water, threw the package out as far as she could, hoping it would stay at the bottom, or that the river would carry it away.

Singing Bird's body drifted down river. The rushing water tossed and turned her lifeless body as if it were a fallen branch. Her long black hair gathered leaves and twigs as it flowed wildly in the rushing flow.

Running Doe could not dismiss the memory of long black hair flowing down-river. She had silenced the competition and temporarily eliminated the threat of replacement, but she was sick at heart. Repulsed by her own actions and deeply disturbed by the memory of the tiny sound that came from Singing Bird, she sobbed as she ran toward the riverbank.

As she approached the clearing, Running Doe tried to appear calm. Slowing her pace to allow her heart to relax its beating, she waved to the playful Powhantuwa and her grandparents and then walked into the water. She splashed her face, so it would appear as if she needed to refresh from her walk. Seeing a splatter of blood on her garment, she walked a little deeper into the river and washed the soiled spot.

Powhantuwa ran to her mother. The two played and splashed for
a while. Running Doe was glad for the opportunity to be away from the adults for a few minutes. She was afraid she could not hide her guilt and shame.

Later, Moon Dancer returned but did not explain where he had been. He did not need to do so. He was the chief. Though the thoughts of sleeping with Moon Dancer repulsed Running Doe, she needed him to love her again. Powhantuwa had satisfied her parental needs but had not met the paramount need of Moon Dancer. As much as he loved Powhantuwa as a daughter, she could not sit on the back of a horse as chief.

Running Doe's thoughts were that, because Moon Dancer knew nothing of her actions toward Singing Bird, his guilt might drive him to her arms for solace. They could become friends again.

Further, if he steps down as chief, there would not be a need for him to produce a future chief. She worried about her own survival.

Remembering a previous incident, Running Doe realized she had a legitimate reason: Once, she, Moon Dancer and Powhantuwa were walking along the river. Powhantuwa was dragging a tree branch, making designs in the sand. To anyone, the scene would look like a relaxing family outing. However, Running Doe could sense Moon Dancer's displeasure. Finally, he asked, "Running Doe, what is wrong? Do you not want a boy child? Have you not prayed to the Great Spirit to give us a son?"

Moon Dancer's accusations appalled Running Doe. Ignoring that they were walking with their child, she yelled at him, "Is this all my doing, Moon Dancer? Do I not give you my body any time you want it? Do you not see me in prayer by the Prayer Rock? I want to give you a son or a daughter of your own! I know you need a son. I know you need to provide for a future chief, but why am I the only one at fault? Does it not take two people to create a child? If we must now blame, could the fault be in you?" Running Doe knew she was in trouble.

Instantly, Moon Dancer stopped the walk, whirled around, and slapped her across her face. She fell against a large log. Powhantuwa screamed, "Running Doe! Oh, Running Doe!"

Moon Dancer was furious that Running Doe would have the nerve to challenge his masculinity. He was the strong and sexual chief of their tribe but hearing the cry of his daughter and seeing the blood on the face of Running Doe, caused him to be more sorry than angry. He picked up Running Doe and carried her to the Healing Elder to doctor her wounds, apologizing as he ran. Powhantuwa ran along behind him, crying. Memories of blood dripping from the face of her mother haunted her for a lifetime.

Moon Dancer was sorry for his actions. His lust for Singing Bird and his desire for a son overshadowed his logic and integrity. His guilt and the attempt to hide his own grief, made him appear insincere.

Running Doe was guilty of killing Singing Bird, but she hated Moon Dancer for his lack of concern. The guilt of taking the life of a girl so young, especially one she loved and nurtured, haunted her. The deception, of which she and Moon Dancer were both guilty, tortured her. They each had their own sordid secrets. Powhantuwa never discussed the incident with them, but they suspected she told her grandparents.

CHAPTER SEVEN
A Mother's Tears

S inging Bird's grieving mother spent many hours crying and praying for her daughter. No one had seen the young girl for several days. Chief Moon Dancer sent braves out into the forest and into other villages, in several attempts to find her. He reasoned that Singing Bird was ashamed after their encounter; and because she loved and respected Running Doe, had gone deep in the forest and took her own life.

Singing Bird had disappeared from the face of the earth. The tribe searched for many days but never found her body. Her mother continually walked the edge of the forest, hoping to find a trace of her.

Every night she sat by the fire and stared through the flames. She longed to hold her child, or at least to have her body to offer to the Great Spirit on a burning bed. The sounds of her crying at night resonated throughout the village. She was without a mate or other children to comfort her. She quit eating and seldom spoke to anyone in the village. One morning, someone discovered her hanging from a tree in the forest. Her grief caused her to risk eternity with the Great Spirit. She gave up her mortal life.

Running Doe's lack of pregnancy was playing heavily on the mind of Moon Dancer. He avoided her. She was sure he was bedding other women. She did not care, but afraid her life depended on the production of a son. She contemplated stealing a canoe, taking Powhantuwa with her and trying to work her way to a distant shore. She knew no tribe on the Eastern Shore would grant her asylum. Her fear of the deep waters, of the Shanaquoix, and the safety of her daughter kept her from leaving her home. The dream that Moon Dancer and Running Doe once shared was falling apart with each passing day. Once, she suggested that he could choose an orphaned boy and call him a son, as other chiefs had done. He told her, "I will pass the leadership to my brother before I do that. He has sons!" His statement struck a sick chord in Running Doe. She never mentioned it again.

The days felt longer. Running Doe kept busy to the point of exhaustion, hoping sleep would come at night. The thoughts of suicide entered her mind more often. Day by day, it became clear that she and Moon Dancer were staying together for appearance's sake.

The tribe needed the assurance of a future chief. Moon Dancer, true to his statement, was seriously considering passing Choptank leadership to his younger brother, White Horse, who had two sons: Manakouk, the oldest and his younger brother, Wamquwa. Both young men were old enough to mate and were two potential future chiefs.

The love that Running Doe and Moon Dancer once enjoyed had finally deteriorated. Because of guilt, they were showing hatred for each other. Running Doe hoped his stepping down as chief would give them peace to rekindle their love.

CHAPTER EIGHT
Powhantuwa's Friend

At age ten, Powhantuwa was doing her share of chores and playing with her friends. She spent many hours listening to stories of her people from her grandfather, especially of her parents, Young Wolf, and Little Fox.

Blue Cloud was always careful to speak of the Powhantuwa Tribe only when he and Powhantuwa were alone. He had willingly declared himself a member of the Choptank Tribe. Powhantuwa would often lovingly take her grandfather's hand and whisper to him, "You are still a great chief. I am your people."

One day, when the tribe was in the assembly, Powhantuwa sat with her grandparents by the Prayer Rock. Suddenly, she felt compelled to look up from the drawings she was creating in the sand. A young girl stood near her. The young girl said, "You are beautiful. I am happy you are here." Powhantuwa smiled as if she knew the person.

The young girl waved and walked behind the giant rock. Powhantuwa waved back to her. Little Bird, thinking Powhantuwa was acting disrespectfully by waving her hand in the air during the tribal meeting, cautioned her to behave. Powhantuwa lay against her grandmother's shoulder and smiled, quietly remembering the 'Pretty Girl.'

Many months passed. One day, Little Bird sat in the warm autumn sun, weaving a blanket. Powhantuwa sat nearby, as Little Bird worked the threads like a musical instrument. Finally, she said, "Little Bird, the pretty girl said I am growing beautiful. What do you think?"

Little Bird stopped weaving. She stared at her granddaughter and said, "Yes, you are, but what girl do you mean?"

Powhantuwa answered, "The one by the Prayer Rock. I see her there." Little Bird asked, "When did you speak to her?"

Powhantuwa answered, "just before I came to you. That is where we talk. She likes me. I like her. She shows me the pattern of the Powhantuwa Tribe. She draws it in the sand. I will weave a Powhantuwa blanket but do not worry, Little Bird. I will not wear it among my Choptank family. I will not offend them. I will wear it only when I sleep at night."

Little Bird asked, "Are you sure your grandfather did not draw you the pattern, and show you the Powhantuwa colors?" Powhantuwa said, "No. she told me the colors."

Little Bird asked, "Where is your loom?" Powhantuwa gave no answer. She smiled and kissed her grandmother.

The heart of Little Bird quickened. She knew the spirit of Little Fox was haunting Powhantuwa. She wanted to discuss her theory with someone, but not Blue Cloud. His time of grief had gently passed. She did not want to stir up sad memories. She went to Hoquia, sister of Running Doe, with her questions. She asked,

"Do you think Powhantuwa is creating the girl in her mind because of the stories of Blue Cloud? Do you think I should speak to him of Powhantuwa's words? Do you think Powhantuwa has always seen the girl?"

Hoquia, who always cautioned her people to be kind to the good spirits, said, "If the spirit of Little Fox is still with us, she is here for a reason. I feel sure no harm will come to Powhantuwa. The spirit of Little Fox visits the area of the Prayer Rock where she died. She waits there for her daughter to come to her." "If the spirit appeared to Powhantuwa when she was a young child, she would not know whether it was real or a vision. When she became the age of reason, she could communicate with the spirit. Yes, I believe the spirit of Little Fox is with us and visits Powhantuwa from time to time. She will only remain until she feels Powhantuwa no longer needs her. We do not know when that will be. I feel she is here for a reason. We need to trust the Spirit."

Hoquia agreed that Little Bird should not speak to Blue Cloud about the haunting, at least for a while."

Powhantuwa grew in beauty and wisdom. Even as she became a pre-teen, she had the maturity of an adult.

Most girls learned how to weave and cook, to bear babies and tend children, and to be a good mate. Powhantuwa wanted all these choices but also wanted to learn of her Powhantuwa ancestry. She also wanted to help her Choptank people grow stronger as a tribe.

It did not surprise Little Bird that Powhantuwa created a loom and wove a blanket with the pattern of the Powhantuwa Tribe, but not convinced of the source of the instructions. She knew Powhantuwa loved her Choptank family and knew the ways of the tribe but felt a responsibility to leave at least a small legacy in memory of her people.

Blue Cloud did not know of a special blanket. Powhantuwa kept her promise to use it only for night sleep. Little Bird suggested they wait to tell him about it after more time had passed. Hoquia kept silent about the matter. Powhantuwa continued weaving with the other girls, but with the Choptank pattern.

Little Bird supposed the haunting remained, but over time, Powhantuwa ceased to mention the pretty girl. She grew into a strong, responsible teen, sometimes acting as an arbitrator for her parents. One day as Little Bird sat staring at the river, the teenager, Powhantuwa, came and knelt in front of her. She asked,

"Little Bird, why do you and I have such sad hearts for my parents? I do not know what to do for them. I cannot understand what has happened to them. One sunrise they love each other, by moonlight, they hate each other. Have the evil spirits taken their souls?"

Little Bird understood Powhantuwa's statement. The tension between Moon Dancer and Running Doe had overshadowed any joy that Powhantuwa brought into her life. She spent much of her time sitting in meditation for them.

Impressed by the maturity of Powhantuwa, Little Bird said to her, "I pray to the Great Spirit for the souls of my family. I pray for White Horse and Moon Dancer alike. I pray for the Great Spirit to do what He would do for our people. I do not question. What He says to do, I will do. If I can only pray, then I will pray."

While they were in conversation, Blue Cloud joined them. He looked down at the two loves of his life: his only relative, Powhantuwa, and his special friend, Little Bird.

Powhantuwa noticed the gentleness between her two grandparents. Theirs was a wonderful relationship and had lasted for her entire existence. She left them to their private conversation.

CHAPTER NINE
The New Chief, White Horse

Blue Cloud took the hand of Little Bird and helped her to her feet. They walked along the shoreline.

He had heard part of the conversation between her and Powhantuwa. He said, "Little Bird, I am also concerned for the parents of Powhantuwa. They hate each other. I am not sure what the spirits are saying to them. I want to say to them, 'If you are to be the parents of my granddaughter, I must know you have a love for each other.' Is this what I should say to them, Little Bird?"

Before Little Bird could answer, Blue Cloud continued, "I try to be kind to Running Doe. She smiles at me as if I annoy her. What did I do to her, that she should be so blind to my affection?" Little Bird had no answers, except to remind him that Powhantuwa was near mating age and would soon not need adoptive, or any parents. She was sure her grandson, Wamquwa, had eyes for her and was a potential mate.

Little Bird said teenager Powhantuwa had dreams of standing in a circle of flowers in the sand, next to her mother, hearing the chief, her father, declare her the mate of Wamquwa but the conflict between her parents clouded her dreams.

They discussed the comparison between the families of her two sons, Moon Dancer, and White Horse. White Horse and his two sons, Manakouk and Wamquwa, were content in their lives. Little Bird said she noticed Moon Dancer appeared to be jealous that Powhantuwa was spending so much time with them. Blue Cloud was sad at her comments.

Moon Dancer was sure his many indiscretions were common Knowledge and that he had brought on the pain of separation to his family. Disturbing thoughts raced through his mind. If he had not forced his power as chief over Singing Bird, she might still be alive. He shamed her by taking away her virginity. It played heavily in his heart; he was responsible for her mother taking her own life. The memories of his errant act continued to haunt him. He observed his brother and his two sons; thinking life would have been simpler if White Horse had become chief.

Not wanting to relinquish his title, but admitting, only to himself, that he could be the barren one, Moon Dancer considered drugging Running Doe, having a young man of the tribe impregnate her, swear him to the secret, and then kill him to keep that secret. He thought of the idea, with pros and cons, wondering if she realized what he had done, and what would happen to their relationship if she found out.

He continued his selfish thoughts, "Would she be able to love the son? What if it was not a son? What if she did not get pregnant? Would he add to his guilt by trying again?" Realizing the irrationality of his cruel thoughts, he went away to the Great Waters to meditate.

One day, against the advice of his brother to take at least one escort, Moon Dancer left the village and traveled alone to the *Great Waters. He visited with the chief of the area tribe. The other tribes considered them brave to live near the end of the earth. He asked for permission to be alone to meditate near their jumping spirits. The chief granted him privacy.

Unlike the earlier visit with Running Doe and Hoquia, when they played at the ocean's edge, he sat in respect for the holy water and the jumping spirits. He sat on the shore, but at a safe distance, letting the water wash past him. After two days of deep meditation, Moon Dancer came to his senses. He begged for forgiveness from the Great Spirit, repented, and took responsibility for his own actions. He even contemplated confessing his adultery to Running Doe. He felt cleansed by the splashing water; his soul was at peace. When he returned to the village, he called a special assembly.

Running Doe wanted no part of any meeting, but the elders required tribal members to attend. Walking alone to the meeting, she tried to lift her mood by daydreaming of better times with her mate. She reminisced about one wonderful day during a meeting by the Prayer Rock, when Moon Dancer announced his choice for a life companion: Moon Dancer's father, Red Wolf, had gone home to be with the Great Spirit.

As the eldest son, young Moon Dancer was the new chief and needed to take a mate. He summoned the tribe to the Prayer Rock, where he declared that Running Doe was his choice. Running Doe stood, joined him, took his hand, and smiled.

During the next full Moon, several friends of Running Doe took her to the river for her ceremonial bathing. After they cleaned her, they put herbs and flowers in her hair and massaged her body with oils. They tossed flower petals on the ground in front of her as she walked up the shoreline to meet Moon Dancer.

The young couple stood in the sand, in a circle of flowers. After chanting, the Medicine Man, who was also the Spiritual Leader, declared they were one. A loud party followed.

Running Doe smiled at the remembrance of that day. However, sad memories of a tree limb crushing the skull of Singing Bird and reverberations of a tiny moan, quickly replaced her sweet reverie. Her sin incessantly haunted her. She hated Moon Dancer for his part in it. Grabbing her churning belly, she tried to dismiss her recollections. Suffering a headache and nausea, she arrived just in time to see Moon Dancer raise his hand. He did not wait for her as he had done in the past. Members were sitting in front of the Prayer Rock. Moon Dancer began his speech. With his new repentance set aside, his self-serving temptation set in, "You all know of Running Doe's failure to give me a son. I am sorry for her failure. I am too old to find another mate. So, I have also failed you."

Running Doe was numb with humiliation. Her friends were embarrassed for her. She resented him for holding her in such low regard, thinking he could not be the weaker one, unable to produce a child. She knew the reason for his stepping down as chief was his guilt. She could tell no one. Telling his secret would reveal her own. She knew he felt unworthy but would not admit it to his tribe. She wondered, "How could he be so cruel and selfish. How could he sacrifice me to the evil spirits?" She angrily turned on her heels and walked away.

The years of suppressed anger and guilt played wickedly in the heart and soul of Running Doe. She ran from the beach. Powhantuwa started to go after her, but Blue Cloud grabbed her. He said, "Let her go. She needs to be alone now."

Powhantuwa cried for her mother. Suddenly, she saw a different Moon Dancer. She asked her grandfather, "How could he be so cruel to his mate? What turned him into such a cruel person? He was once so kind. Does he hate me because I am not a son, or that I am not a true Choptank?"

Blue Cloud answered, "Moon Dancer does not hate you. He hates himself. He has told me about many things. You do not need to know the things of the older ones. Just believe he loves you as his daughter. He has just lost love for Running Doe because she has not given him a son. Running Doe is sad about that, but she is powerless to do anything about it."

Powhantuwa heeded the words of her grandfather. She walked back to the meeting in time to see Chief Moon Dancer remove his Head Dress and place it on the head of his younger brother, White Horse. She saw Running Doe standing in the distance, watching Moon Dancer removing himself as chief, then walking away. Her hopes of him stepping down as chief was no longer important. Their dream was over.

Little Bird sat with her head down, crying for one son, praying for both and happy for the tribe. At least one solution was in place. She knew, under the circumstances, and despite his sadness, Moon Dancer's decision was good for the tribe.

Moon Dancer hid his grief long enough to complete the rite of passage. When he finished speaking, everyone cheered. They knew of the bitterness between him and Running Doe.

A fresh beginning was the mood of the day. People danced, chanted, and showed allegiance to their new chief, shouting, "Chief White Horse. Chief White Horse"

The new chief raised his hand. When all was quiet, he told his people, "My love for the Choptank and reverence for my brother, has brought me to this day? I will be your chief. My brother, Moon Dancer, will be by my side. You must be kind to him as a brother. He loves the Choptank. He is stepping down as chief because he wants what is best for our people. He knows he cannot lead as chief while he is ill."

After hearing the words of White Horse, the members conversed with each other and each resolving to be kinder to Moon Dancer. They did not know he was ill. Moon Dancer had confessed his sin and repentance of adultery, in confidence to the new chief and to the religious leader. Therefore, White

Horse knew in his heart that his words were true. Moon Dancer and Running Doe were both sick people. They were in deep despair. Running Doe never confessed her sin.

White Horse continued, "My two sons, Manakouk and Wamquwa, stand ready to lead you when I go to be with the Great Spirit."

The villagers were happy to have a new chief. They were wary of the tension and obvious hatred between their former leader and his mate. They resumed their chanting and dancing, but their attitude of prayer changed. They were now praying equally for Chief White Horse and Chief Moon Dancer. The celebration continued well into the night. Powhantuwa, resisting the impulse to look for her mother, went to her sleep.

Moon Dancer was no longer the Pretend Chief. However, he realized, with his accusations against Running Doe, he had, once again, grieved the Great Spirit. He deeply regretted his recent actions and tried to ease his pain by drinking more fermented berry juice than he should. When he could no longer dance, was having trouble talking and could barely walk, he left the celebration.

Stumbling, he went to look for Running Doe. He knew she did not want him to find her, but in his drunken stupor and regardless of his previous accusations, her safety concerned him. He walked the beach until he reached a large bed of rocks covered with piled up tree branches and leaves. He collapsed to rest on the rocks and fell asleep. The heat of the morning sun and the peal of water splashing on rocks awakened him. He staggered to his feet and called out for Running Doe. There was no answer.

Being sick from the previous night's indulgence, Moon Dancer made a gut-wrenching sound and regurgitated on the rocks. Then, climbing over his own vomit, he continued his search for

Running Doe. In his semi-drunken condition, he did not even consider that she could be back at camp.

Reaching a familiar edge of the forest, he realized he was heading toward the area where he took the virginity of Singing Bird. He fell to the ground and sobbed. He was no longer a big chief. He was a guilt-ridden, broken, hurting soul. He cried, "Singing Bird, where are you? Many moons have come and gone since you were with us, yet your spirit haunts me still. Where are you? Where are you?" He was not grieving for Singing Bird, but for his own sanity. He could not accept that she had left the tribe. He needed assurance that he did not cause her death. He stumbled deeper into the forest. He could no longer hear the river. He almost passed out. Suddenly, he saw Running Doe sitting on a nearby rock. She was, temporarily, saddened at his drunken condition. Thoughts of their childhood, their courtship, and their union played in her mind. She ran to him, crying, "Moon Dancer. Oh, Moon Dancer."

Moon Dancer cried back to her, "Do not be kind! Do not be kind! I have grieved the Spirits! I caused the disappearance of Singing Bird. It was me! It was me! I caused her death. I caused her mother's death. It was me! It was me! I could not bear to tell you." He continued to sob.

An instant memory of Moon Dancer in his Forest Love Bed and his recent humiliation of her played before the eyes of Running Doe. She was angry that he came to her with contrition in his heart when they had no love or respect left between them or any way to salvage any part of their life together. His confession was an abomination to her. All these thoughts seemed like one giant ball of disgust, causing her to attack him with vile words of hatred. She beat him with a large limb from a fallen tree, screaming, "I loved you! I loved you!"

51

Moon Dancer exerted no effort to defend himself. He wanted punishment. Running Doe continued to beat him with the tree limb, screaming, "Moon Dancer, I heard you. I saw her. It has been many moons and I still hear you in my sleep. I hear sounds of you and Singing Bird being together. I could not let her live." Moon Dancer stared in horror and disbelief, barely believing her words.

Another time, Running Doe would have been afraid to touch Moon Dancer, or even speak to him in anger. Even the peaceful Choptank would not tolerate insubordination. That day she did not care if she lived or died, so she had no fear.

Running Doe's words of confession were too repulsive for Moon Dancer. For a while, he could not say a word. He was in shock and in great pain from the severity of her violent blows against his body, especially his head. The thoughts of his mate murdering such a beautiful young girl sunk into his already sickened soul. He yelled at her, "You knew all this time, and you did not tell me? You watched me suffer in anguish many suns and moons, yet you made love with me and did not take the blame for Singing Bird's death! You let her mother suffer until she died.

You said nothing! You are worse than I am! You are a murderer! You should have killed yourself long ago, instead of letting others suffer!" Running Doe said, "Do you not know I was suffering too? I cried for Singing Bird every sun and every moon. I prayed for forgiveness but never got it. I wanted to kill myself but did not for the love of Powhantuwa."

Moon Dancer raised his hands. He yelled, "Stop! Do not use the name of Powhantuwa. She is unblemished. You do not care for her. How could you be her mother and teach her the ways of our people? You are a murder…"

The words were too much for him to finish. His head was pounding and bleeding profusely; his blood splattered against a nearby tree and on Running Doe. His left ear was partially severed. He was in extreme pain and let out a screeching scream. The horror of what his mate had just screamed at him created a violent rush of blood to his head. With vehement force, he grabbed the tree limb from her hands and using it as support, pulled himself up to face her.

Running Doe stood motionless as Moon Dancer's tall frame, one that once stirred a wonderful passion deep in her soul, loomed over her. Moon Dancer let go of the tree limb and grabbed her by her shoulders. He screamed at her, "It was you! You were the evil one! You let me wonder and suffer so much guilt for many seasons!" He angrily repeated, "You are the evil one! She was a child, a beautiful child!"

Running Doe screamed back at him, "Yes! She was a child. You put evil spirits in her soul! She was no longer good for any brave!" Moon Dancer just stared at her. He knew she was telling the truth. Still, he felt a loathing for what she had done. Running Doe knew Moon Dancer would kill her but showed no resistance. She wanted to die, to escape her torment.

Emotions were swirling around and through the couple as if arrows were piercing their bodies and stabbing at their hearts. Their joint betrayals had brought them to a state of hatred and sorrow. They knew their actions had surely saddened and offended the Great Spirit. Then, suddenly, as if by divine providence, a sorrowful longing for their lost love surrounded them. The emotions were over, under, on top, and in the depths of their souls.

Moon Dancer loosened the grip on Running Doe's shoulders. He looked lovingly at her. His tears joined the blood on his face.

Running Doe looked up at him and cried, "Moon Dancer, I'm so…" Moon Dancer interrupted, "No. You are a good person. You tried to do right by me, by our people. You are a good mother to
Powhantuwa. She will be a good person because of your teaching. I caused you to do what you did. I blamed you because I was too proud." Running Doe said, "We have offended the Great Spirit. We must go to our new chief. I will confess my sin. He will forgive me; send my body to the flames and my soul will be with the Great Spirit. You will be free to start a new life. Powhantuwa will have a new, cleaner life."

Moon Dancer dropped his aching head. Running Doe caressed his face. He returned the gentleness. A renewed love and compassion arose in them. Their caresses progressed into a frail, but genuine passion.

A weak Moon Dancer put his arms around Running Doe. While attempting to lower her to the ground, his head exploded in pain. He fell against her. Running Doe's head landed on a sharp-pointed rock. She moaned softly and closed her eyes.

Moon Dancer grabbed her body. He moaned and chanted for the love of her. He fell on her breast, sobbing. He tried to shake her back to life. Running Doe was barely breathing. She opened her eyes. Suddenly, Moon Dancer and Running Doe saw a vision of Singing Bird walking through the forest toward them. It terrified them, but they were too weak to run away.

In the vision, autumn leaves were falling around Singing Bird. She looked young and pretty. The tortured couple waited for condemnation. They received none.

The spirit of Singing Bird stood over them. A gentle wind surrounded her, causing her long black hair to flow in the breeze. At first, her countenance was one of pleading. Then, it changed into gentleness, as if she knew of their pain. She came closer and gently reached out to them. Forgiveness was in her eyes. The air was still. No birds were chirping. No animals were running through the forest.

There were no sounds, except for the gentle music playing from afar. A silent fear encompassed the couple. As the music came closer and closer, the fear gradually and tenderly disappeared.

The spirit of Singing Bird raised her hands as if in prayer. She ascended. Looking back at the couple, she beckoned them to follow. She flowed past the clouds, toward the river. Eventually, she disappeared. The cursed couple had desperately needed forgiveness. Finally, they felt peaceful. The Great Spirit had recognized their repentance. Singing Bird was the messenger.

Running Doe took a quick gasping inhaling breath and never exhaled. Then, with bloody tears in his dark eyes, and with a sigh, Moon Dancer also took his last breath and joined her in death. The sounds of nature, resonating through the woods, muffled the couple's final moans and sighs. The morning sun glistened through the trees. Dew moistened the greenery.

A canoe, powered by the oars of two young braves, moved smoothly on the river. The sounds of water flowing by the rocks at the shoreline echoed loudly. The fragrance of wildflowers encompassed the riverbank. Birds were diving into the river, capturing their breakfast, and flying off to devour their catch.

The Osprey watched from its perch high in the trees. Rabbits, squirrels, and other small critters scurried along the morning paths, seeking their morning meal. Fish were jumping in the beloved river.

A soft breeze blew through the forest, gradually changing into a cleansing windstorm. Trees were forcefully swaying. Critters scurried to find shelter. Tall green grasses along the river were falling into the water. Dry grasses swirled around and around in the fields.

The Great Spirit was cleaning house. As quickly as it began, the storm was over. The trees stopped swaying.

A gentle calm embraced the peninsula. Most of the tribe did not even notice the turbulence, because they were asleep. The combined sights and sounds of nature told the world that life was good again, and all nature was continuing as it always had.

A quiet serenity encompassed the cove where Singing Bird left the earth. On a nearby bush sat a small bird, singing a peaceful lullaby.

The river flowed smoothly. It was, again, at peace. Birds were chirping. Music was in the air.

Life was anew along the Choptank.

CHAPER TEN
On That Same Morning

For most of her life, Powhantuwa had been the catalyst for her parents. Her grandparents were the major constant in her life. Moon Dancer's behavior the previous night confused her and weighed heavily on her mind. After having a restless night since her parents left the council, she was finally sleeping. A nightmare awakened her.

Remembering her dream:

Powhantuwa smiles as she hears music and watches the dancers. Moon Dancer is her handsome father, and she reveres him as her chief. Moon Dancer smiles as he dances around and around in the joyful reverence for the Great Spirit. His beautiful Running Doe looks so young. They smile at each other. He takes her hand. They walk past Powhantuwa without speaking and continue walking toward the river.

Powhantuwa tries to touch Running Doe, but Running Doe appears to be rising to the clouds. Powhantuwa cries, "Moon Dancer, Help her! Help her down. Bring her to me. I can heal her. I can heal her!"

Moon Dancer turns to face Powhantuwa. With tears running down his cheeks, he sadly shakes his head. Powhantuwa is frightened because she has never seen her father weep.

Moon Dancer ignores the words of Powhantuwa. He stretches his hands toward Running Doe. His hands disappear in the fog of the morning mist. His body follows his hands, going up and up to the clouds. Powhantuwa runs as fast as she can to reach her parents, but as she looks down, she realizes she is still standing in the sand by the Prayer Rock. The river serenades the happy couple, "Swoosh, Swoosh, Swoosh."

The music is growing louder and louder. Powhantuwa screams, "No! No. Bring them back. Bring them back!" Her own voice awakened her. Trembling and crying, she sat up. Trying to calm, she thought, "Just a bad dream." She had them before. Somehow, that dream was different. It seemed so real. She trembled as she rose. She was yet to hear of her parent's deaths. She had a serious reason for concern.

Earlier, on that same morning,
Blue Cloud sat by the morning fire, trying to mediate. His heart was heavy. He lowered his head, held it in his two hands, and wept. He was ashamed, for this was not the actions of a chief. His heart was full of sorrow and pain. Even while Powhantuwa was having her dream, he was in prayer.

He prayed, "Oh Great Spirit, please reveal what you want me to know this day. I come to you for your blessing. I pray for our people. I pray our hunters will bring good food to the evening fire. Please allow our children to find joy as they play on the warm sands of your blessed river. I pray I will please you with my obedience. Please bless my friends, Running Doe, and Moon Dancer, and especially my dear Powhantuwa."

He chanted aloud, but quickly stifled his voice, so no one would hear him. His heart was racing, and his soul was troubled. He wondered if Powhantuwa was in danger. However, he was a devout man. He trusted in the love of the Great Spirit. He forced himself to say aloud, "I will bless this day. I will not let the evil spirits steal my joy."

Powhantuwa approached him. With a forced smile, he said,

"The day's beginning is a holy time. The Great Spirit smiles on us, and we smile back. We are one. What a beautiful sun, the Great Spirit has given us, Powhantuwa."

Powhantuwa gently embraced her grandfather, but her heart was heavy with worry. She asked, "Have you seen my parents, Grandfather?" Blue Cloud answered, "No, not this day." He repeated, "Not this day."

Trying to avoid conversation about his friends, Blue Cloud moved the firewood closer into the flames. He talked about the harvest and the coming winter. Powhantuwa kissed him and walked to the river.

On that same morning,
Little Bird, concerned since Moon Dancer left to find Running Doe, waited until she thought all the members had gone to their sleep, then she went back to the Prayer Rock. She wanted to be alone to pray for her family. She sat slightly at an angle, facing east, so the Great Spirit would see her face in the morning light. As she prayed for her family, a vision, one she had experienced years before, appeared to her.

Little Bird's Vision:

The river is flowing wildly. A girl's voice calls out, yelling, "Help me! Help me!" Little Bird is sure Running Doe is in danger. She jumps in the river. As she nears the 'voice,' spiraling water pulls her down. The more she follows the voice, the deeper it pulls her into the abyss. As she descends, she sees many, many strands of long black hair floating over her, forming a cloud so dense she can no longer see through the blue water. In a panic, she reaches up to move the hair away. As she does, the vision ends.
Little Bird's mind returned to the present. She trembled at the

memory of her vision. She knew in her heart it was a sign of great sadness.

On that same morning,
White Horse, the new chief of the Choptank, joined Blue Cloud by the fire. He said, "Blue Cloud, I do not want to say this to the tribe, especially to my mother, but I fear for my brother and sister. The spirits tell me to search for them. I do not want to. I fear for what I will find. Last night, I hoped that they would find each other and be together. I hoped that they would find their lost love and return to us as loving parents for our young Powhantuwa."

White Horse continued, "My mother is a devout woman. I would like to ask her to tell me what the spirits are saying to her, but I do not want to cause pain in her heart. I still pray to the Great Spirit for peace with Chief Moon Dancer and his mate. I pray the spirits will let this be so. I call on you now, my friend, to be my advisor."

The words of the young chief saddened Blue Cloud, but he smiled at the reference of Moon Dancer, as chief. He knew White Horse loved and revered his older brother and had not wanted to become the leader of the tribe by default, and, at his brother's expense. He said to White Horse, "My friend, I spoke my prayers to the Great Spirit with a heavy heart. I also fear them. There is much trouble in their hearts. I hope that they are talking in peace about their new life." He repeated, "But I fear for them."

Much earlier, on that same morning,

Even before Blue Cloud and White Horse sat by the fire, and Powhantuwa and Little Bird were having their visions, Manakouk, son of the new chief, shook his younger brother. He commanded, "Wamquwa, Wake up. Hurry! We must find Moon Dancer and Running Doe. They did not return to the council. I had a dream about them. I looked for them. They are not in their tent. They are not in our village. I cannot find them."

Wamquwa rubbed his tired eyes and jokingly said, "Manakouk, why do you look for them? Why do you worry? Could you not see Running Doe needed comforting last night? Moon Dancer is comforting her now. We should just leave them alone. They will return when they are ready. Moon Dancer needed time to grieve. He is no longer chief. That is upsetting to him. Let him be."

Wamquwa tried to go back to sleep, but Manakouk shook him and continued making a blanket roll. As he was tying it, he said, "I cannot believe you, Wamquwa. My Spirit Guide has awakened me with such thoughts. They must be true. Get up and go with me."

Wamquwa usually never questioned his brother's intuition. This time, he did not want to believe their aunt and uncle were in any danger. He believed they were simply renewing their love, but he quickly obeyed his older brother. They quietly enlisted young hunting trainees as a search party, and went out early, before the villagers awoke, to look for the couple.

Manakouk knew the beach and shoreline of the river had always been the choice for serenity walks for Running Doe and Moon Dancer, so he began the search there, walking along until a large pile of rocks and branches broke the path. Moon Dancer had drunkenly used the same rocks as a bed. The early morning rain had eliminated any evidence of his visit there.
Manakouk and Wamquwa led the search party up the bank to go around the rocks and then back down again to the shore.

They continued their search along the beach and only slightly in the forest.

Manakouk was sure if they found Running Doe, it would be along or near the water. He secretly feared that she had walked into the river. He had a special love for his Aunt Running Doe. He admired her endurance: First, losing her parents at an early age, and then raised by her strict older sister, Hoquia. Over the years, he realized she had lost her joy of life, appearing sad most of the time. As the search party continued along the beach, his mind was capturing a picture of a happier time. He remembered:

One day when he was young, Manakouk watched Moon Dancer smile across many heads to select young Running Doe as his mate. He remembered that Running Doe beamed as she stood, and how Moon Dancer looked adoringly at her as they danced. He asked aloud. "What happened to their love?"

Wamquwa asked, "What?" Manakouk answered, "Nothing." His thoughts were, "If only they had a son, if only…" Manakouk quickened his pace. Then, as if the spirits were directing him, he pointed toward the forest and walked at a faster pace. Wamquwa knew not to question his brother's judgment. Manakouk believed in his Spirit Guide. Therefore, when he motioned for the search party to follow, they, including Wamquwa, quickly followed.

Manakouk was at a running pace. By then, Wamquwa felt the spirits were directing his brother's path. Manakouk suddenly stopped his jog, dropped his head, and wiped his sweating face. He had labored breathing. For a moment, Wamquwa feared an evil source had taken control of his brother. He asked, "Manakouk, are you still with us?" Manakouk nodded as he sat on a log to rest. He quietly motioned for the others to sit. They obeyed. After a few minutes, Manakouk regained his composure. He quietly instructed the trainees to tread as quietly as animals as they approached the more densely wooded part of the forest. The young men, remembering their training, obeyed. Suddenly, they heard the obvious sound of wild animals growling. Manakouk held out his right-hand palm down and then lowered it. The entire search party quietly crouched on the ground. Through the bushes, they saw the horrible sight of wolves gnawing on the bodies of Running Doe and Moon Dancer. It sickened them. Fighting his emotions, Manakouk silently counted eight wolves. His search party totaled fourteen.

The horrible sight before them stunned the younger men. They were subjected to the gruesome action for the few minutes Manakouk took to design the attack.

Quickly, Manakouk, with his left hand, fingers spread representing each wolf and using each finger as a reference, he pointed, pinky to thumb. With his right hand, he pointed to half of the men and then to four of the wolves. They nodded. Quickly closing and opening his hand, he continued his reference, with the second group of young men. They nodded. If anyone missed their target, they would all surely pay with their lives. If they did not kill the wolves: the wolves would kill them. They also knew they needed to kill the wolves all at once. Not doing so would almost guarantee their own deaths.

The wolves already had a taste of blood. They would fight to their death to keep their catch. The Braves were confident in the leadership of Manakouk and were thankful the odds were two to one in their favor.

Finally, at the signal, the group quietly drew their bows. Each brave shot his first arrow with sharp precision into the bodies of the busy wolves. The injured, but powerful wolves charged them.

Seeing the fear in the eyes of the young braves, Manakouk screamed at them, "Fight for your life, you cowards! Fight for your life!" The young men quickly fired more arrows directly into the chests of the charging beasts. Finally, all the wolves were dead. Manakouk was proud of the young shaking trainees. The ordeal was repulsive for them, but they had a dreadful task to complete. Sensing their emotional nausea, he instructed the entire search party to go cut and gather tree limbs to make two burial beds.

The young braves were happy to be away from the mangled bodies for a few minutes. They went out of sight and vomited. Working with the wood helped them temporarily escape the horrifying death scene.

Manakouk and Wamquwa quickly gathered more soil and leaves and spread them over the wrappings to camouflage any remaining smell of human blood. They covered the heads of their aunt and uncle with piles of leaves, to avoid seeing them. They kicked mounds of dirt over the bodies to mask any remaining odor. Finally, they wrapped the bodies tightly in the blankets that Manakouk had the foresight to pack.

The young braves, returning with the burial beds, were glad to see that they covered the bodies. Manakouk sent four of the youngest back to the village to report to White Horse and to gather the tribe for the burial fires.

As Manakouk worked, he remembered seeing his grandmother sitting by the river in prayer as the search party headed out of camp earlier in the morning. She saw him. They felt the same crying spirits. He dreaded seeing her face when the burial beds passed by her. After the group secured the bodies on the burial beds, the remaining braves carried the beds on their shoulder. Manakouk and Wamquwa walked behind them, back to camp.

After hearing the news, Chief White Horse ran to meet them. Upon seeing his father, Manakouk signaled the carriers to set down the beds. The young men obliged and walked a short distance away to allow White Horse privacy to grieve his siblings before he faced the entire tribe by the fire. He especially needed to cry for his brother if only for a few minutes.

White Horse suffered the burden of knowing Moon Dancer's sin. He secretly hoped he had confessed it to Running Doe, and they resolved their differences before being attacked.

Manakouk looked at his own brother, Wamquwa, and realized how painful it was for White Horse. After a few minutes, White Horse signaled, and they rejoined him. White Horse caressed the larger body, and then the smaller one. He whispered, "He was my brother. She was my sister." His two sons nodded.

White Horse only lingered for a short while. He turned; his head held high and walked back to the village. Manakouk signaled the young braves to continue their burden. They picked up the burial beds and carried the bodies to their final soul cleansing: the fire.

The entire tribe had learned of the tragedy and was waiting for them. They could not take time to grieve. They had to prepare for the funeral, give the funeral, and then chant for the souls of Moon Dancer and Running Doe, all on the same morning. Grieving would come later. Powhantuwa stood motionless as men placed her parent's bodies on the high beds.

Chief White Horse stood silently as he lit the fire of Moon Dancer. Hoquia lit the fire of her sister, Running Doe. She stepped back and stared at the towering inferno. No tears surfaced. Her heart was breaking, but her true emotion was one of anger toward Moon Dancer, remembering how he treated her sister. She wondered if he killed Running Doe and if it was premeditated. She wondered if passing on the leadership of the tribe to his younger brother was a part of that plan.

Other questions arose in her mind: Did Running Doe kill herself? When Moon Dancer found her, were the wolves already there? Did they kill him as he tried to keep them away from her body? Did the wolves attack them?

Hoquia was in mourning; her thoughts were running wild, confusing her mind. She sat in prayer for understanding and strength to say goodbye. She knew she also needed to pray for strength to forgive.

Little Bird was inconsolable, her grief overwhelming. She had lost a son and a daughter. She remembered other times and other burning beds: The one for her mate, Red Wolf, and the one for the mate of White Horse, plus many others. She recalled those other fires as she watched the flames.

Blue Cloud sadly remembered the horrible attack on his people. He could not bury his own dead. The Metapoke braves did it for him. That had always saddened him. He remembered the kindness of the Metapoke tribe and the kind words of Moon Dancer, related to him by the chief of the Metapoke. He took comfort in remembering the kindness the Choptank showed him as they welcomed him and his granddaughter into their tribe.

As he remembered a sweet young woman gently placing the Powhantuwa baby in his arms, tears streamed down his cheeks. He cared not. He did not have to be brave. He was no longer the Powhantuwa Chief Blue Cloud. He was a grieving friend. He looked over at Little Bird, then stood and went to her side. She acknowledged his presence but spoke no words. They needed none. She took his hand and gently pulled him down to her side.

When the flames of the burning beds were at a roaring high, White Horse chanted. As protocol dictated, Little Bird, Hoquia, Powhantuwa, Manakouk, and Wamquwa followed. One by one, the members stood, danced, and chanted. They offered prayers for the lost lives and for their peaceful journey to the Great Spirit. The prayers continued until the flames consumed all the flesh.

The beds burned and fell to the ground. Their fires turned to embers. The same young braves that had fought the wolves, sifted through the cooled ashes to recover the bones of their chief and his mate. Then, respecting the customs of their ancestors, White Horse and his family buried the bones of their loved ones in the field behind the Prayer Rock.

Wamquwa held the hand of Powhantuwa as she took her last walk with her parents. She remained only long enough to add her stones to their graves. Then she went into seclusion to grieve. She was, once again, an orphan, but she was no longer a helpless child by a cold rock. She was a vital person, a survivor, old enough to become the mate of a young brave, yet young enough to need her mother's arms. Although the deaths of her parents would sadden her, she was free of the exhausting attempt to be a loving channel for their love.

Harvest was near completion. The tribal members had stored crops as food for winter. Warm autumn leaves covered the ground. Children were enjoying wonderful games of falling on the golden cushions. White Horse summoned his two sons to meet with him. As they ate their noon meal, he spoke, "Soon, the chiefs of the other tribes will join us to reaffirm our pact to protect this land. The other chiefs will leave their strongest and older braves to guard the northern land. There will be young braves traveling with them. Those young braves will have eyes for our young girls."

Manakouk nodded. He knew of the meeting. He was overseeing the preparations for the visit. Women were gathering food and cooking to feed the large assembly. Children were practicing their dances. Gifts for the visiting chiefs were already on display, so he questioned a special meeting with his father. White Horse stated, "You know we allow anyone to leave the tribe in peace if they wished to go."

Manakouk smiled as he remembered the young girls being giddy over the visiting young braves. He acknowledged his father's information, then asked, "But Father, why do you tell us such things today?"

White Horse asked, "Is there anyone who has become ready to mate, who you wish for a life companion?" White Horse was sure of the answers but wanted to be fair to his sons in letting them choose their own mates but, his question took the two brothers by surprise.

Manakouk loved a young girl, Hatsawa, but no ceremony had taken place to declare her womanhood. He had not approached her. Wamquwa played the field. He cared deeply for Powhantuwa and thought she might be the right one to choose for a mate but felt that because she was in mourning for her parents, she may not be ready to do the sexual duties required of her.

The brothers expressed their concerns. White Horse considered their issues. Then he continued, "I say this to remind you that one of you will someday be the chief of our tribe. As the chief, you must have a mate who will bear you a son. The young braves who will be here with their chiefs may not have chosen a mate. They may look at our young girls. If you have one you claim, do it to keep her from being declared eligible."

CHAPTER ELEVEN
Couples

Manakouk and Wamquwa had both gone on their *Vision Quest* and were qualified to mate and/or become chief of their tribe. The next step was to choose a life-mate. They surely did not want to lose the girls whose affection they had encouraged for most of their lives.

*masculine, proving time alone in the wilderness

That was the romantic atmosphere embracing the brothers as each left to propose to the girl of his dream. Manakouk had grown into a strong young man. As the future chief of the tribe protocol dictated that he had a mate to produce another future chief. Putting all of this aside, he had eyes for Hatsawa. She was interested in him. As children and pre-teens, they often fondled each other; but had remained celibate. Protocol had nothing to do with Wamquwa making a choice. He always planned to mate with some girl, someday. Chief White Horse had speeded up the process.

Manakouk and Hatsawa

It was a beautiful warm autumn day. Manakouk walked through the village looking for Hatsawa. Finally, he found her washing a blanket at water's edge. He stood and lovingly admired her for a few minutes, ashamed that his father had to force him to approach her.

He walked up to her and clumsily asked, "Hatsawa, have you become of mating age?" Hatsawa, appalled at his question, threw the wet blanket at him, and stormed away, toward the village.

Manakouk, wet and startled, asked the sky, "What is wrong?" Hatsawa angrily turned to look at Manakouk. Seeing him soaking wet with the draped blanket, she laughed. Manakouk, realizing how humorous he looked, laughed. Hatsawa walked back to him and knocked him down. They rolled repeatedly on the wet sandy blanket, teasing, and tossing each other.

Finally, the laughing couple came to a rest. Hatsawa raised her head and rested on her elbow with her face in her palm. She asked, "Manakouk, why do you ask me such a question? You know I had my run." Manakouk clumsily answered, "Because the full moon will visit us soon. On the next sunup, I want to take you for my mate." Hatsawa asked, "So, why do you not just ask me?"

Manakouk smiled and said, "So now I ask."

Hatsawa laughed and hugged Manakouk. After assuring him she was of age and agreed to his request, she reminded him, "We must go now and ask the chief for a flower circle."

Manakouk teasingly smiled and said, "I'm sure White Horse will be pleased and will allow our union." Secretly, he wanted to bypass the ceremony and make love to her immediately, but Hatsawa was a special person in his life. He wanted their life together to begin as a perfect union. He helped her finish washing and wringing the sandy blanket before going to the chief for his blessings.

When they arrived at the tent of White Horse, Blue Cloud and Little Bird were there. White Horse waved the younger couple away. Deciding next day would be soon enough to speak to the chief, Hatsawa went back to her laundry.

Manakouk walked into the woods.

Powhantuwa's River

Wamquwa and Powhantuwa

Though Wamquwa had strong feelings for Powhantuwa, he was not sure he was ready to make a commitment to one girl. He loved the attention he got from the young girls of the tribe. His father would permit him to have only one partner.

He knew that Powhantuwa always wanted him to belong to her. As they grew, he randomly returned her affection. Although he enjoyed spending time with other girls, he kept her close in his sight. He selfishly wanted no one to put a claim on her in case she became his choice. She was mating age, but the chief delayed her ceremonial run because of the deaths of her parents.

Wamquwa needed to make a choice for a mate. Encouragement from his father inspired his decision. She was a natural choice.

A few days after the farewell of Moon Dancer and Running Doe, Powhantuwa, who had been in seclusion since her parent's funeral, finally ventured out into the day. Even then, she spent most of her day sitting alone, staring at the river.

One warm afternoon, she sat recalling the wonderful times she had there. She loved hearing the story of her brave birth mother; how she died to save her. Sometimes, she felt guilty that her mother died bringing her to the Choptank Village. However, she knew if her mother had not made that arduous journey, she, herself, would not have survived. Throughout her life, she continually asked the Great Spirit to bless her spirit mother.

That day, she prayed fervently for the spirits of all her parents. Though she was in no mood to pray for anyone but herself, she forced chants for many other concerns. The absence of parents and the responsibility of prayers propelled her into maturity. She knew her own existence was Blue Cloud's salvation and his reason for healing. That awareness gave her small solace. She was exhausted. The call of the river and the gentle answer of nature served as a lullaby. Mentally fatigued and warmed by the autumn sun, she fell asleep.

Wamquwa stood on the bank of the river, looking at the beautiful sleeping young woman; her long tresses fell seductively over her face and shoulders. He smiled, as he remembered their childhood and her obvious infatuation for him. Although he loved her as a cousin and friend, he never really appreciated her wonderful character until that season of her parent's death. He admired the maturity with which she conducted herself during her parent's funeral and the logic of solitary retreat to grief.

Being moved by the sleeping Powhantuwa and being sexually aroused by her beauty and new sensual appearance, he sat down on a large boulder and continued to watch her sleep, telling himself that he was protecting her. The simple reason was his youthful lust. His pulse quickening, his dominant desire was to take advantage of the situation: to awaken her with an embrace, take her into the woods, and seduce her. Her honor was not the determining factor that kept him from doing so, rather, the wrath of his father and older brother.

With these thoughts and unsatisfied lust, he left Powhantuwa to the warm afternoon sun and walked into the woods.

Later in the week, Powhantuwa was walking along the shoreline. Wamquwa joined her. When they reached the small cove where Singing Bird left the earth, Wamquwa stopped walking.

Powhantuwa stopped walking. She looked up into the eyes of the young brave she loved. She had always worried about his affection, or lack of, for her and had almost given up the hope he would consider her for his mate. He had always been kind to her, but because many young girls shared his affections, he never appeared especially interested enough in her. Yet there he was, walking alongside her, behaving like a lover.

Finally, Wamquwa spoke, "Powhantuwa, I know it has only been a little while since Moon Dancer and Running Doe have crossed the river, but it is time for me to choose a mate. I will wait, but if you would like..."

Wamquwa's words were inaudible. Powhantuwa was not sure if he was nervous or insincere. It confused her. He did not function as if he loved her as she wished, but that did not keep her from being thrilled at the prospect of sleeping with him. She wondered if he selected her for his life mate, or was she the choice of the chief? She could barely believe the question when the words finally came out of his mouth. She thought, "Would I?"

With words finally formed, Powhantuwa said, "Wamquwa, I have always loved you. I thought you did not love me. You have always been kind but..." With her voice trailing off, she wept.

Wamquwa spoke again of his concern she might not be happy sleeping with him while she was still grieving her parents but reminded her that the time of the full moon was near. He wanted to become her life partner.

Powhantuwa gently put her pointer finger to his mouth and said, "Wamquwa, I need you with me. I have always wanted you. I need your arms to comfort me at night, now more than ever. I need your body with me when I sleep. I will try to be a good mate to you. I will try to satisfy your desires and give you many sons."

The bold statement from Powhantuwa electrified Wamquwa. He had never heard her speak so freely about her feelings for him. For a moment, her boldness staggered him. He took her hand from his mouth, turned it over and gently kissed her palm. He investigated her gentle and passionate eyes as if seeing them for the first time.

The height of emotion that arose in Wamquwa, on the day he watched her on the riverbank, could not compare to the ultimate arousal he experienced at that moment. He took unauthorized liberty of caressing her lips with his own.

The kiss grew into an embrace; the embrace led to a deep desire for each other. That desire exploded into passion.

Wamquwa drew Powhantuwa close to him. They were both in a state of overpowering emotion and surprise at the height of desire between them. They clung to each other.

As a silent gesture of acceptance, Powhantuwa took Wamquwa's right hand and placed it on her breast. They stared into each other's eyes. He continued to caress her body until she moaned quietly in his ears. She stood on tiptoes and slowly kissed his neck, and finally, his broad shoulders. He looked down at her. She was smiling.

The splashing water, carrying loose floating twigs and branches in and out of the small hidden cove, created an undeniable rhythmic invitation to love.

They strolled into the woods.

CHAPTER TWELVE
Flower Circles and
Morning

On a warm autumn day, under a tranquil blue sky, the tribe gathered on the beach and banks of the Choptank River. Fragrant flowers adorned the sandy river edge. Children were running around with flowers and playing with stems left from the cutting of flower heads. Babies were crying. Mothers were tending them. Young girls were standing around, dreaming of their future-mating day.

On that golden autumn day, by the river he loved, the proud Chief White Horse chanted. The tribe joined in the chant. The evocative rhythm of the drums and the chanting of the approaching young braves escorting Manakouk and Wamquwa to the flower circles brought cheers from the waiting crowd.

Children, throwing flowers, danced in front of Hatsawa and Powhantuwa as they walked to the beach. The chief instructed the two couples to join hands and step into a Flower Circle. After they did as he commanded, the chief raised his hand high, signifying "Quiet."

Powhantuwa looked for her grandparents. Afraid that something had happened to them, she thought, "I cannot go through this ceremony without them."

Chief White Horse interrupted her thoughts, "We wait." It relieved Powhantuwa. She thought, "Oh good. We will wait for them." Thinking the chief was just biding time while they waited, she watched as he took flowers from the hand of a child. The members wondered why he motioned for the children to gather more cut flowers and join him. The children obeyed. He dropped more flowers on the sand. They did the same. When they finished, they had created a third circle between the existing two.

As the chief chanted again, another couple, Blue Cloud and Little Bird, walked hand in hand on the sand, from the south shore toward the gathering. When they finally reached the crowd, the chief motioned for them to step inside the center circle. The older couple smiled and obeyed. The crowd loudly chanted with approval.

Blue Cloud proudly held the hand of Little Bird. Powhantuwa cried with joy. She looked up to the clouds and whispered to the spirits of her parents, Moon Dancer and Running Doe, Young Wolf, and Little Fox, "I have love. Please be at peace." She knew the spirits of her parents, the four of them were happy.

When the spiritual leader declared Wamquwa and Powhantuwa were one and he could take her to his bed, Wamquwa smiled and squeezed Powhantuwa's hand. She stood as a composed 'virgin' should and gently smiled at him.

Chief White Horse blessed the couples, one by one. The ceremonies only took a few minutes. The celebration continued long into the night.

When the moon was at its brightest, the villagers threw the flowers into the flowing river. The flowers danced with the flowing, splashing waters. Life was looking good again for the tribe of the Choptank. It had been a perfect day.

The gentle spirit of Little Fox walked quietly along the sandy banks, away from the celebration. Her long, silken, black hair flowed gently with the breeze. She smiled, opened her hand, and released five little berries. As she watched them disappear into the blowing wind, she whispered. "It is good we came here. It is good, my little one. You have grown into a beautiful woman for your brave mate. He loves you. I am happy. Now I will leave you. When you join the Great Spirit, I will see you again." Tears filled her eyes, but they were tears of joy. She smiled again and slowly walked away.

The next morning,

Manakouk and Hatsawa watched the children practice their dance for the Powwow of Nations, Hatsawa pointed to them and teasingly asked, "How many of those do you want, Manakouk?"

Manakouk smiled, pulled Hatsawa close to him and said, "Many. Many."

Hatsawa thought, "Watching children dance is not my choice for this first day." She then reasoned that Manakouk would be chief someday and already had many responsibilities. She wanted to be his faithful companion. Throughout the day, they went from one activity to another.

The meeting of tribes was only a few days away. There was much to prepare. Hatsawa understood Manakouk's responsibilities. However, she wanted to be courted, at least for a few days. She was pleasant to Manakouk but was not happy with her post-wedding day.

Finally, in the golden evening, when the day's activities had ended, Manakouk took her hand and led her away from the crowd. They walked by the river as they had done so many times before.

As they reached a small cove, away from the village, Hatsawa smiled. There, before her, was a private, romantic wedding banquet, complete with a blanket, food, and drink. Manakouk took Hatsawa's hand and helped her to the blanket.

Hatsawa laughed as she settled down to their feast. She said, "Manakouk, you are sweet. Now I know why you kept me so busy. This is a pleasant surprise." Manakouk answered, "Please do not tell that to the others. They think I am stern." She promised.

They enjoyed their evening well until dawn. If Hatsawa knew Manakouk had a safety patrol stationed around the perimeter, she would not have enjoyed her evening as much as she did; and would have been a little quieter.

What a Glorious Morning.

Powhantuwa arose early and went to the river. She looked up to the sky and joyfully sang out, "How can I be so happy? He loves me. He really does!" She jumped onto the river's edge and playfully splashed the water. Feeling energetic, she sat and rubbed her heels in the sand. She looked out to the middle of the river and asked, "Are you rejoicing with me, oh waters?"

Suddenly, she discarded her garment and jumped in the water. Disregarding the rule of avoiding the deeper part of the river, she swam out as far as possible, giggling as she swam. The middle of the river was moving swiftly. The current forced her along with it.

Fortunately, a fallen tree functioned as a dam. grabbed a limb and clung to it for a few minutes to gain her composure. The giggles changed to gasping.

Wamquwa stood watching his new mate. He picked up her garment and ran along the riverbank, preparing to jump in and save her, but felt she was learning a valuable lesson. He would not hinder a tutoring session by Mother Nature. He walked down to a shallow inlet where he knew she would come ashore.

When Powhantuwa got out of the water, he stood nearby, holding her garment. He tried to look stern, but the image of her flapping and grabbing at the tree limbs was playing in his mind. He was laughing inwardly at the sight.

Powhantuwa said not a word but looked into his eyes. He handed her the garment. She took it from him, dried her face with it, and pulled it over her head. She let it fall slowly over her body. All the while, her eyes stayed fixed on his. Wamquwa said nothing, but walked to her, took her hand, and led her into the forest.

The Hum of Morning awakened Little Bird.

The inviting aroma of the morning meal penetrated the wedding tent. The chirping of birds sounded like a serenade. She looked over at the sleeping Blue Cloud and smiled at the memory of their Flower Circle and ceremonial dancing. She remembered her son, Chief White Horse, putting his hand on the shoulder of Blue Cloud, and declaring him as his father. As she lay there, she had another memory of the previous night:

The celebration is over. The river of wedding flowers in the moonlight was a beautiful sight. The other recently mated couples had long gone to their tents. Blue Cloud and Little Bird were enjoying the remaining warmth of the glowing embers. Blue Cloud took the hand of Little Bird. He did not speak but looked at her tenderly. Little Bird smiled and said, "Blue Cloud, we have been friends since you came to our village, many moons ago. I am so happy I am now your life partner. Why are you so quiet?"

He stood and held out his hand to help her to her feet. They walked. He finally spoke, "Little Bird, you are right. We have been friends for a long time. I am an old man. I did not think before I asked you to mate with me. I am afraid I will lose your affection if I cannot be a good sleeping partner."

At that memory, Little Bird caressed Blue Cloud's gray hair. Deciding to let him sleep while she bathed, she quietly slipped out of their bed, put on her garment, raised the flap of the tent to step out.

She paused, looked back and quietly whispered, "Blue Cloud, my best friend, you have nothing to worry about." She smiled and walked quietly to the river.

CHAPTER THIRTEEN
Birth of Manassaquoit
(Mann-a-squa)

One year after the wedding ceremonies. Hatsawa was pregnant with her first child. Powhantuwa had not conceived a child. At first, it concerned her. She enjoyed having Wamquwa as a companion and felt the Great Spirit had granted them time to grow closer. However, watching Hatsawa caress her belly from time to time, she worried that she, herself, might be barren.

Hatsawa was excited about her pregnancy but one night she awakened from a nightmare: In her dream, she saw her son who was still in her belly. He was a tall, proud, handsome man. He was on a horse. An arrow came from the bushes and pierced his heart.

Hatsawa cried, "Ooha, Ooha." Manakouk woke her. She was in a trance. She cried to Manakouk, "The spirits show me we will lose our son to the evil one. I am looking down from the clouds." Manakouk held her while she cried. Concerned by her vision, about the one of her looking down from the clouds, Manakouk tried to comfort her, saying, "It is just your time. The waiting makes your head crazy. You will see."

Trying to be reassuring, he said, "the Great Spirit has already smiled on you. We will have a strong son. We will live long together to see him grow. Just a bad dream."

Being calmed by the man she adored, Hatsawa fell asleep. She stayed in a sleepy state until long into the new day when a sharp pain in her belly awakened her. The pain subsided. Powhantuwa brought food. As they ate, Powhantuwa said, "Hatsawa, you are older than me. Both of my mothers are dead. I do not wish to speak to Aunt Hoquia or to Little Bird until later." Then she asked, "Can you talk with me?"

Despite her discomfort, Hatsawa granted the request. She asked, "What is it?" Powhantuwa answered, "How do I know the Great Spirit has smiled on me? How will I know I am to have a son to give Wamquwa? I do not know even when to tell Wamquwa or Little Bird, even if I am with child." Hatsawa smiled. She did not know Hoquia had not described the symptoms of early pregnancy.

Powhantuwa knew about babies. She had even assisted in some deliveries. Yet, she felt unsure of her own abilities to know when, or if, she was pregnant, or when should she reveal it to Wamquwa.

Hatsawa always enjoyed her quiet visits with Powhantuwa. However, that day she needed to postpone their conversation. A cramp that had begun deep in her belly earlier in the day had become full-fledged pain. That pain was increasing minute by minute. She sat up.

Trying to sound brave, Hatsawa announced, "Powhantuwa, I will tell you what you need to know on the next sunup, while I am feeding this child who is trying, **just now**, to enter our world!"

A sharp pain sent her body to the onset of labor. As she began delivering the future chief of the Choptank Tribe, she screamed aloud, "Ooha! Ooha!"

Powhantuwa cried, "Hatsawa, I am so sorry, I did not know. I did not know! What do you want me to do?" Hatsawa grabbed the arm of her 'little sister,' dug her fingers into its flesh and through clenched teeth ordered, "Get help! Get Hoquia. Hurry!" Powhantuwa ran from the tent, yelling for Hoquia. Sweat was pouring down the forehead of Hatsawa as she got into a squatting, childbearing position. She managed to utter a prayer to the Great Spirit, and to any ancestors who could give her aid. She whispered, "I am ready. Please smile on me, oh spirits of my people. Help me." With those last words, she gave out a wailing, screeching sound, "Ooha! Ooha!"

Hoquia, Powhantuwa and a few young women reached the tent as Hatsawa and her guiding spirits, brought Manakouk's son into the world. Hoquia sent the young women away and then aided Hatsawa and her new son.

Tribal tradition dictated that the father would name his child according to the first thing he saw when the child was born.

During the pregnancy of Hatsawa, Manakouk had often sat by the Prayer Rock, watching, and talking to a giant fish eating 'river eagle,' an 'Osprey' who nested with his mate high in a tree overlooking the river.

Manakouk decided he would fix his eyes on the osprey's nest, so it would be the first thing he would see when he heard Hatsawa screaming in labor and, especially, when he was sure his son was in the world.

Manassaquoit (man-a-squa) was a name Manakouk had given to the giant osprey. He had never touched the bird but had claimed it as his pet. He did this several months before when he learned of the pregnancy of Hatsawa. He did it for the sole purpose of choosing the right name for his first-born son. He wanted a majestic name. He was sure his first-born would be a boy.

When he heard the first pre-labor sounds from Hatsawa, he ran to the Prayer Rock. There he sat with his eyes closed, pledging that he would only open them when he received word of the birth. If the child were a girl, he would quickly look away and let nature provide a name. He would save the name of Manassaquoit for the next (boy) child. It was a form of cheating, but he felt justified. His first-born son would someday be the chief of their tribe.

On that day, when Manakouk heard the full sounds of labor from Hatsawa, he faced the tall tree, so he would be looking at the formidable wonder of nature when the baby entered the world. His constant prayer had been that the bird would be visible to him when he heard of the birth of his 'son.' He closed his eyes and chanted for Hatsawa, and for the safe delivery of their child. Happily, the giant eagles were in the nest.

Manakouk was proud when he heard of the birth. It was a son! He was a father and his Hatsawa was well. He opened his eyes and stared at the nest. He kept his eyes fully fixed on it until the giant bird was fully in focus to him. He said, "Manassaquoit, my Giant Osprey, I thank you for giving me a name of my first-born child."

Manakouk summoned everyone to the Prayer Rock, then he went to his tent. He kissed Hatsawa as she slept and then took the baby outside. He chanted to the Great Spirit in thanks for the safe delivery of his first-born son. He held the boy-child overhead and declared its name to the tribe,

"This is my son, Manassaquoit.

CHAPTER FOURTEEN
Journey of Chief White Horse

When Manassaquoit had been on the earth for three years, Manakouk and his younger brother, Wamquwa, answered a summons to join their father, Chief White Horse.

The chief was the first to speak, "It has been almost four seasons since we have not had Moon Dancer as our chief. We have had no problems with the Shanaquoix (sha-nock-qua) because many tribes are guarding our land.

Our young braves are taking turns guarding our territory, but they should not be away from their families during such long missions for this protection. I want to make talk with the new Shanaquoix Chief and try to get his tribe to be a willing member of the alliance. We need a peace agreement with them. This is the right way. We will prepare to go to their village."

Manakouk said, "Do you think the evil tribe has become peaceful just because they have not attacked us? I do not. They are evil spirits. We are a small nation compared to them." Wamquwa agreed but wished for a peaceful existence, so he kept his negative feelings to himself.

Manakouk asked his father, "Will we take them many gifts? Will we send word ahead? How do we prepare for this talk?" Chief White Horse spent the rest of the conversation telling his sons of his plan. He explained that he made the decision, so it was his responsibility to enter their village. He said he would hold a flag made from white feathers to show his peaceful mission and felt certain the Shanaquoix would allow him to enter their village in peace. White Horse explained that Manakouk was next in line to be chief and needed to stay in the village to protect the tribe if the plan backfired, causing the Shanaquoix to become wild through the land. He had already sent a request to the other tribes in the alliance, to meet with him. He promised to discuss his plan with them.

White Horse said if the other chiefs did not support him, he would forget the plan. Manakouk did not like the feeling arising in his spirit. Although Manakouk respected White Horse as a compassionate brave, wise chief, and father, he questioned his judgment. He sat in silence, considering his father too optimistic concerning any peace talks with the Shanaquoix.

White Horse sensed that Manakouk was apprehensive about his decision; he motioned for him to stay for a moment after Wamquwa left. He said, "Manakouk, do not grieve the spirits about my decision. I know you worry about your brother. I will not cause harm to come to him. Do not fear. When we reach the Big Water, I will command my escorts to stay and wait for my return. I will go to the other side alone to speak to the chief of the Shanaquoix.

"Wamquwa and the others will be safe on our side of the water. Many braves will patrol and be guarding the land. They will all be standing strong as protection. I feel certain the chief will see *****I come in peace. No harm will come to me. Be strong for our people, my son." Manakouk answered, "I am also concerned for you, my father. I fear that harm will come to you, and I am not sure you can manage a large canoe in the Big Water." Manakouk looked at his father and knew there was no further discussion.

Disregarding the aged old belief that the Big Water belonged to the Good Spirits; White Horse would attempt the crossing alone. He ordered the construction of a large canoe he would use to cross the deep water. He ordered a feast for the meeting of chiefs.

The next day the members of the alliance met at the village of the Choptank. They sat around in a large circle. There was, as usual, a lot of food, dancing, and merriment. After their meal, White Horse presented his plan. At the end of the meeting, all the chiefs agreed a peace talk was a possibility. They each offered to accompany White Horse, but he reminded them that many braves might appear to be a war party to the Shanaquoix. White Horse said it was his idea. He would not request others to join him. He did not tell them of his plan to go the last leg of the journey unescorted. Manakouk stood silent, deeply disturbed, as his father spoke. He knew White Horse would be alone when he faced the Shanaquoix.

A few days later, young men set a new, large canoe on a rugged carrying bed and secured it with ropes; they left long ends hanging for pulling the bed. After all preparation were in place, several men mounted their horses, each holding a rope. At a signal, they pulled the canoe. White Horse predicted the trip would only be one or two days. He told his young daughter-in-law, Powhantuwa, "I will bring Wamquwa safely back to you."

Blue Cloud was disturbed that White Horse would enter a village of a tribe he, himself, considered devils but reasoned that a previous generation had conducted the annihilation of his tribe, and for the benefit of the eastern shore inhabitants, he hoped a truce with the new chief was possible.

Hoquia, the older sister of Powhantuwa, stood, disapprovingly, with her head down. As she watched the small parade leave the village, she feared White Horse had made a poor decision.

After the second day, Manakouk had the same thoughts but kept them to himself. He did not want to worry everyone. Powhantuwa barely slept. Hatsawa tried to keep her occupied. The two 'sisters' usually spent their afternoons with Manassaquoit in the same cove where Running Doe slaughtered Singing Bird, but they had no way of knowing that fact. It was a blessing the spirits had kept those visions from them. Manassaquoit was an energetic young boy, big and strong for his age. Hatsawa was swollen with another child. She was sure she would give Manakouk a daughter. Powhantuwa was finally with child, and due to give birth about the same time as Hatsawa.

The two young women delighted in that fact. Over time, they and other girls in the village had many talks about signals and symptoms of pregnancy. Powhantuwa was anticipating the new phase of her life with joy. She wanted to bear the child of her lover, Wamquwa. The two young women shared their joy daily. Hatsawa would often laughingly tease, "We are giving our people their leaders." Powhantuwa would laugh and agree.

One morning: the third day of the Peace Talk journey, the young women were relaxing in the cove. Manassaquoit was learning to swim. Hatsawa caressed her belly and said to her unborn child, "I know you are my little girl." She stood, stretched, smiled at her swollen reflection in the water, and then struggled to sit back down on the rock. Both women giggled at her attempt and at their conditions. Manassaquoit splashed them with the cool water. They played and laughed.

After Manassaquoit showed his swimming ability, he came out of the water and hugged his mother. Hatsawa said, "You are my big strong brave, Manassaquoit." Instantly, she had a reoccurring vision of him in danger. She shook it off as a mother's fear. As they prepared to go back to the village, they heard the parade of horses. "They are back! They are back!" shouted Powhantuwa. She ran to greet the returning party.

Hatsawa and little Manassaquoit moved a little slower than her. They arrived just in time to see her falling faintly to the ground. It confused Hatsawa, for she clearly saw Wamquwa. Manakouk turned to her and said, "Take the boy to his sleep!" Hatsawa stood in shock for a moment. Manakouk, who had never spoken sternly with her, and out of character, angrily repeated his demand, "Hatsawa, take the boy from sight. Put him to sleep. A horrible thing has happened. I do not want him to know it. I will share it with you when you return."

Hatsawa wanted to tend to Powhantuwa but obeyed Manakouk. She was grateful that Manassaquoit was sleepy from his swim and soon fell asleep. She covered him with a light blanket and walked out into the light. Little Bird was sobbing and convulsing in the bushes. Her family was trying to console her. Instantly Hatsawa knew something had happened to White Horse, for he was not with them. Hatsawa approached them with questioning eyes.

Manakouk guided her away from the gathering crowd. He controlled his emotions long enough to relate Wamquwa's story as Wamquwa told it to him. He spoke quietly, "The words of Wamquwa: "We arrived at the edge of the Big Water. White Horse told us to dismount but to stay near our horses, on our land. I begged him to let me go with him, but he refused. We could not persuade him to let some of us go with him. He ordered us to stay on our land. We put the canoe in the water.

White Horse struggled to manage it alone but rowed it out to the deep and gained control. He went to the other side of the water. He was in the Shanaquoix Village for one sun, then one moon. We rested. At the next Sun, two large canoes, full of braves, approached our edge of the water." We did not see our canoe. One brave from each canoe stepped into the shallow water to come to us. I did not see White Horse. I asked for him.

One brave spoke. He said, 'These are not my words. These are words of my chief. He says we no longer want your land. We will stay on our land. You stay on yours.

Our chief ordered us to come to you. If we do not do as he says, we are dead. If you harm us and we do not return to our chief, our tribe will be wild on your land in the night while you sleep. We will be wild in all your villages until we leave no one. This is the word from our chief. Now, we return to our village. You stay on your land.' "

Wamquwa continued his report, "I asked them for our chief. The two braves spoke not a word but got into their canoes. We stood, wondering what to do. We had no canoe to follow them back to their land. The Big Water was too deep for our horses. As the Shanaquoix braves began paddling their canoes out to the water, we were yelling, asking about our chief. One brave looked right at me. He seemed to want to speak but did not. He tossed a sack at my feet. I opened it. In it was the head of our father! Only the head! Only the head."

As Manakouk spoke, Hatsawa clasped her hands over her mouth. Her head exploded in tremendous pain. Grabbing her own belly, she screamed, "Manakouk, I do not want you to be chief! I do not..." He had no words to console her, for he was inconsolable. They held each other and sobbed. Blue Cloud held Little Bird as she grieved. She had lost a second son. She moaned, "I should go to be with the Great Spirit, not my sons. Not my sons!"

On that fateful day, Manakouk became the new chief of the Choptank. The men built a funeral fire bed to send the soul of White Horse to the Great Spirit. Even if the members were in emotional pain, it would not sound like it, because the chanting and dancing became louder and louder. The drumbeats became wilder as the sun set The moon was waiting to give light to the tired, grieving people.

CHAPTER FIFTEEN
Birth of Tucahaunna and Shaahatuck
(Tuck-a-hauna) (Shh-ha-tuck)

Amid the clamor of the funeral day were other sounds: the recognizable, unforgettable sounds of child birthing.

While the sun was still giving light, Hatsawa and Powhantuwa both went into labor. Both babies were struggling to come into the world while the smoke from the burning bed of White Horse was still covering the river's edge. Both women hid away from the crowd behind the Prayer Rock.

Blue Cloud reminded Little Bird that it was fitting for Powhantuwa to give birth by the same rocky area where Moon Dancer found her when she was only a few days old. Little Bird declared, "That is a good sign from the Great Spirit for this time." Blue Cloud knew that even in her grief, Little Bird would chant and pray to the spirits and rejoice in the life of her family.

Hatsawa gave birth to her second son. Manakouk named him Tucahaunna, which meant father. He chose that name because he was having visions of the spirit of his father, White Horse, the baby's grandfather, as Tucahaunna was born.

Hoquia was busy tending to Powhantuwa when Hatsawa was giving birth.

Hatsawa should have taken priority, for she was the mate of the chief. However, she motioned for Hoquia to support Powhantuwa. Other young women were competent in aiding her. Powhantuwa clumsily sat in a squatting position as

Hatsawa had taught her. She was quickly introduced to the pain of childbearing as the infant within her struggled to enter their world. She was tense from the death of White Horse, his immediate funeral, and the fear of childbirth. She could not relax and have her baby as nature intended.

Little Bird approached the back of the rock. She heard Hoquia, unsuccessfully, trying to aid Powhantuwa in the delivery. She said to Powhantuwa, "This child's grandparents need to be happy. We want to hear the cry of our grandchild, so we can chant for joy. The Great Spirit will help you drop this child in my arms. I will sit and wait while you pray." Her words were simple.

Powhantuwa was ashamed. Her grandmother had just experienced grief no mother should ever have to endure, yet there she was, more unwavering and loyal than anyone could expect.

Powhantuwa panted and pushed with a flawless rhythm, yelling, yet laughing. With a loud cry, she gave birth to a beautiful baby girl. After the birth, Hoquia cleaned the baby. She and Little Bird took Powhantuwa and her new child back to her tent. Other women supported Hatsawa.

While Little Bird helped Powhantuwa's birthing, Blue Cloud sat alone by the river. He chanted a prayer of thanks to the Great Spirit for the birth of his great-grandchild.

Although the Powhantuwa Tribe was almost extinct, Blue Cloud was content. The thought of a grandchild, a wonderful symbol of his ancestry, gave him a sense of worth.

An emotionally exhausted Little Bird walked down to the riverbank. Blue Cloud was waiting for her. He had such loving respect for her. He knew she would not sleep for a while; knew where she would go, and that she would need his comfort. Little Bird was also sure where she would find Blue Cloud. She managed to smile as she approached him. Seeing her, he stood and took her in his arms. They held each other without speaking.

Finally, Little Bird said, "Hatsawa has a son. Powhantuwa has a daughter. When she was pushing the baby girl from her body, I was talking to her, but I was seeing my two little boys. I remembered them falling into the arms of my mother as they came out of my body. I could see them, later, standing with their father, Red Wolf. They were smiling proudly, after catching their first fish out of this river. My memory of their deaths is clouding the happy ones.

"My sons are gone. Blue Cloud, the pain I feel is like the one you bear. If I do not have you, I think I would just walk into the river and not come out. I would make the river grass my bed. I would just close my eyes. I am so happy you are here with me. Please stay with me until I cross the river and go to the clouds."

Little Bird's words touched Blue Cloud's heart. He could barely speak. He closed his arms more closely around her small frame and said, "Little Bird, when you cross the river and go to the Great Spirit, I will go with you."

The exhausted couple stood by the refreshing water for a while, letting the sun warm their faces. Then they went to their bed. They slept the rest of the day and into the next morning.

Manakouk and Wamquwa felt that Chief White Horse had died dishonorably. They had no physical body to send to the Great Spirit. Knowledge of that fact caused them severe grief. It concerned them about the mental health of their grandmother. Both of her sons suffered violent deaths.

The day of White Horse's funeral was bathed in diversity for the brothers. The day began with heartache, but the births of their children gave them solace. They prayed, in thanks, as devoutly as possible, to the Great Spirit. Later, Wamquwa loved to tell the story of the moment of his daughter's birth, "I was sitting under a tree on the bank of the river after the burning of my father's burial bed, praying for the safe journey of his spirit. Powhantuwa gave birth to my child. I prayed for her and for the child. Suddenly, a tiny bird fell, or pushed from its nest. It rested on my lap and died in my arms. I caressed it while I chanted. When I could enter the tent, I showed the tiny bird to Powhantuwa. She also caressed it. I put the tiny bird in bed with Powhantuwa and the baby."

"The spirit of the tiny bird entered my child and became her gentle spirit. I told Powhantuwa that I named our baby daughter Shaahatuck because it means a tiny bird. She agreed and was happy. I took the tiny bird outside, built a small fire and burned its body so it could live with the Great Spirit, and would watch over my little daughter."

Little Bird was an elated great-grandmother, because the name Shaahatuck, (tiny bird) was so close to her own name. She felt Wamquwa named his beautiful little daughter Shaahatuck because her completed name, Shaahatuck-akanna could mean 'Tiny Bird by the Rock.' That was how she came to be a part of their life:

She was their little Shaahatuck.

CHAPTER SIXTEEN
Needed Closure

Blue Cloud looked at Little Bird; at the slight wrinkles that appeared around her eyes as she squinted in the late day sun. He took her hand. They walked without speaking. The splashing water and answering echo from the rocks was a romantic love song for the older couple. They walked along the entire shoreline until they reached a rock piling. They sat on the rocks for a while, enjoying the view. The birth of their great-granddaughter had created an even greater bond between them.

Blue Cloud released his hold on Little Bird, picked up small stones, and tossed them into the water. She laughed and did the same. Disregarding their advanced ages, they played as children. Little Bird took a small stone and caressed Blue Cloud's back with it, causing a yearning sensation to run through his body.

Little Bird said, "Now our blood runs through our granddaughter. We are truly one." She laid her head on his shoulder and said, "When I feel your heartbeat, I am close to you, even more than the first day. I am content." Blue Cloud smiled, put his arm around her, and pulled her closer to him. He said, "What you say is true. I am content here with you and your people." Little Bird corrected him, "Our people." Blue Cloud smiled and nodded. They sat in silence and listened to the sounds of the early evening but, Little Bird had learned her mate's body language enough to know something was on his mind. She waited patiently for him to speak.

Blue Cloud picked up a twig and drew in the sand. Finally, he stated, "Little Bird, when I was young, my father suggested that

I take Satuwa as my mate. I did not love Satuwa when we mated, but I liked her. We were of the same tribe, knew each other. After we were together, she told me she always loved me. She was a good person. She gave me four sons and one daughter, my Little Fox, Powhantuwa's mother. I had a choice of girls, but I listened to my father. He was a wise man. I grew to love Satuwa. Now I am long in years. I still have a choice. My choice is you."

Tears clouded the eyes of Little Bird. She offered her out-stretched hand. He took it in his hands, turned it over and kissed her palm. They sat quietly for a few more minutes, holding hands and watching the setting sun, and then walked back toward the village.

Little Bird sensed Blue Cloud had more to say. He slowed his pace as if he needed more time to finish the conversation. Finally, he spoke, "Little Bird, I am happy here, with you. Do you believe me?" Little Bird, confused by his statement and question, answered, "Yes, I do. You and Powhantuwa have brought much joy to our village. I am sorry Little Fox did not live to be with us, but why do you ask that of me?"

Blue Cloud answered, "I need to go to my village once more. I need to pray for the spirits of my people before I leave to go to the Great Spirit. I want to ask Chief Manakouk for his blessings to do this thing. More than the blessings of our chief, I need you to know I do not cry for Satuwa. I was happy with her, but it is you I now love but I need to pray for her spirit, for the spirits of our children, for the spirits of the people of my tribe, and for my peace. Do you understand this?" He took her by her shoulders and said, "I need your understanding."

Little Bird smiled at Blue Cloud to assure him of her support. She said, "Blue Cloud, my love for you tells me you should go to your village to pray for your people." Then, as a symbol of total understanding, she said, "The chief of our tribe also chose me. Unlike you, I did not have a choice. I came from a small tribe down the river. We could not survive.

"We had many women, but our men were few. Our chief asked other tribes to welcome us into their villages. Some of our members joined the Choptank Tribe. Many fathers gave their daughters to braves of other tribes. Many of the members with us today are descendants of my old tribe. When we came to live with this tribe, Red Wolf was a new chief who needed a mate. He looked favorably upon me because my father was chief. My father gave me to him."

"When we were still in our village, I was a young girl, ready to mate during the beginning of one sun. Our village celebrated with me. We danced and chanted to the Great Spirit. Then, we came here to this village. My mother had not yet talked with me. She could not speak of such things and said I would know what to do for my mate when the time came. The time came too soon for me to learn anything.

"I was happy my father gave me to Red Wolf. I cared deeply for him, but I cannot say I loved him. I did not know what he expected of me when we became mates, but I trusted him. He was a few years older than me. His father had taught him how to care for me."

Little Bird continued. "After my cleansing, Red Wolf took me for a mate. I liked him; I really did. He was kind. I gave him two sons. I was happy with him. We survived and took care of each other until he went home to be with the Great Spirit. We were friends for all our lives together, but I never thought of loving a man before I saw you. On the day you came to our village with the chief of the Metapoke, I liked your face. When I took the Powhantuwa baby from your arms, I saw tears in your eyes. I felt love for you. I was ashamed of my feelings. I was the old one, mother of the chief, but the feeling would not go away. I had tears in my eyes, and in my soul, because you would leave our village with little Powhantuwa and I would never see you again.

"Later that day when you told us you wished to stay with our people, my belly jumped. I quickly prayed to the Great Spirit to tell all people to accept you. You made me so happy the first time we walked together. I could not stop smiling even when I went to sleep. I thought my son asked you to treat me kindly. He knew I would be a good companion for you. I asked you that question once, remember?"

Blue Cloud smiled and replied, "Yes, I remember." He paused for a moment as they walked. Then he added, "You and I never regarded each other when I visited your village with my father because we had mates. Now I feel I have known you in another life. You have the same spirit as me. Do you think we were once together in another life?"

Little Bird said, "I do not even think of such things. I love. That is all." Blue Cloud squeezed her hand. They laughed and walked up the bank to the village where their families were waiting for them by the fire. Seeing secretive smiles between them, the two young mothers shot smiling glances at each other.

The older couple ignored their inquisitive looks. They smiled, sat, warmed their hands by the fire, and enjoyed their evening meal. Little Bird smiled softly as she remembered her parents, "My parents lived with this tribe until their deaths."

CHAPTER SEVENTEEN
Pilgrimage of Chief Blue Cloud

Chief Manakouk gave Blue Cloud, blessing for the requested journey. Blue Cloud had originally wanted to wait until Powhantuwa was well enough to travel with him but felt he had already waited too long. He hoped they would go later. Little Bird tried to persuade him to let some villagers accompany him. Because of his refusal to her request, and as ridiculous as it seemed, she felt jealous of his dead wife. Blue Cloud was not aware of this. He planned to involve no one in his quest.

Manakouk had another idea. He called an assembly. Once the tribe gathered, he announced, "The Powhantuwa has been a good friend to our tribe. He has brought with him much wisdom. We have learned to grow better food because of his skills. We have beautiful children, Powhantuwa and Shaahatuck, because of his daughter, Little Fox. He has been a good companion for our mother. He has long been with us and will soon go to be with the Great Spirit. So now, he wishes to go to the village of his people, to their graves. He wants to pray for their spirits while he is still on this earth; before he joins them."

The words of her grandson, Manakouk, sweetly touched the heart of Little Bird, for they were true. She and Blue Cloud would soon go to the Great Spirit. She dreaded living without him. She daydreamed of them taking the journey together. Manakouk's next statement interrupted her thoughts, "I have given him permission. Now, I come to you for your blessing and companionship, to travel with him on his journey." At that final statement, Manakouk sat next to Blue Cloud. After a moment, he stood. He remained standing, signaling his support for Blue Cloud. He asked the tribe, "Will you walk with him on this journey?" Wamquwa was next to stand. Soon, the entire tribe was standing. The tribe's affection humbled him. He clung to the hand of Little Bird. She returned his grip.

Chief Manakouk continued, "I will send messengers to the Metapoke, and invite them to join us, for they were the people who saved the life of Chief Blue Cloud. They buried the bones of his people. The Great Spirit heard their prayers for the dead Powhantuwa people, but Blue Cloud could not chant, for he was almost in the clouds. He needs to pray to the Great Spirit. Metapoke will be with us, we will be many and will be safe. We will all go."

Little Bird loved the entire tribe taking the journey together. She was happy Blue Cloud would have a peaceful sleep afterward.

Hatsawa was nervous about taking her two young sons on such a journey so early in the year. She expressed her concern to Manakouk. It was, a damp, only occasionally warm, spring. Berries and fruit were not yet growing.

Manakouk laughed and assured her they had an ample supply of dried meat to suck on, winter squash and plenty of grains. Her babies would not go hungry.

Powhantuwa, not only being nervous traveling with her baby, also trembled at the thought of seeing the place where the slaughter of her people took place.

The knowledge that on the return trip she might travel the same path as her mother prompted an abysmal sensation in the pit of her stomach.

Wamquwa's thoughts angrily wandered back to the earlier

season when the Shanaquoix slaughtered his father. Manakouk constantly reminded Wamquwa to pray to the Great Spirit to ease his pain and ask for guidance for each day with his beautiful mate and daughter. Wamquwa was trying to do that, but the nightmares would not stop. He was having difficulty playing games with his friends or laughing at anyone's stories. He could not forget the sight of the sack, containing the head of his father, that someone tossed at his feet.

Nothing that Powhantuwa, or anyone else, could say or do would ease Wamquwa's guilt and grief. He was not the same Wamquwa. He wanted to show respect and take the journey with Blue Cloud. However, he was severely depressed and secretly dreaded the ordeal.

Manakouk did not notice Wamquwa's anxiety, for he was busy preparing the entire tribe for the journey, securing their village, and preserving their food. He knew wild animals would wander through the abandoned settlement.

Hoquia begged to stay and guard the village. She felt sure her strong will and numinous powers would be enough to deter any wild animals from wandering through their home, but Manakouk would not hear of it. He reminded her. "I made a pledge to Chief White Horse, that when he was no longer the chief, I would always watch over you. I cannot do that if you are not with me. Also, we may need your powers to pray for the Powhantuwa people." The chief had spoken. That was that!

Early the next morning, mothers prepared items for their families. Children were playing. Parents were reprimanding them to hurry with their chores. Members were gathering in a parade lineup.

Finally, the entire tribe began their journey to the abandoned Powhantuwa Village. They used a few horses to carry the supplies and the old members, young nursing mothers, and young children. Most members of the tribes walked.

When the Metapoke joined them, they stopped and rested, ate a light meal of dried meat, fish, and grains, and then continued their journey. A large entourage was going on a mission to ease the spirit of one thankful old man.

Blue Cloud and his entourage arrived at the site of his previous home a few hours before sunset. Entering the village triggered many emotions for him and Powhantuwa.

A few older Metapoke braves remembered the horrible sight of their neighbor's bodies strewn across the village. They sadly remembered the many burial beds they built and burned, prayers they prayed and especially, the cutting down of the dumbstruck chief of the tribe. They compassionately watched him as he stood at the entrance to the abandoned village.

Dark Eagle, chief of the Metapoke, joined Blue Cloud. They walked together for a few minutes. He pointed to an area near a line of trees. Blue Cloud walked alone to the place where Dark Eagle had pointed: the tribal burial place.

Blue Cloud walked around the village. Little Bird wanted to comfort him but knew he needed some time alone. He needed to let it sink in again and then, through prayers, let it go.

Blue Cloud, trying to hide his tears, looked up to the sky. After a few minutes, he walked back to Little Bird. In silence, he took her hand. They walked around the village. He pointed out various places, and told of events, even forcefully smiling from time to time. She held tightly to his hand as he spoke.

While they were walking through the village, other members made a fire and prepared the evening meal.

CHAPTER EIGHTEEN
Destruction of Wamquwa

After the community meal, the celebration began. Chief Manakouk nodded to Blue Cloud. Blue Cloud looked up to the sky, arose, chanted, and danced. Chief Manakouk and Chief Dark Eagle joined in the dance. Many people were chanting and dancing. Hatsawa and Powhantuwa, because of their recent birthing, and their 'travel weakened' bodies, sat with Little Bird.

Wamquwa, who had been drinking more fermented berry juice than he should have, joined in the dance. He looked wild. Suddenly, he stopped dancing. He sat at a distance from his family. It concerned Powhantuwa. She got up to go to him, but baby Shaahatuck cried. She sat and nursed the baby, watching and crying for Wamquwa all the while.

Little Bird declined to join the dance, feeling it was for the other family of Blue Cloud. It was his time. She was content to sit and watch his pleasure as he received the closure the Shanaquoix had denied him. She welcomed the warmth of the giant fire and lovingly watched the dancers. In her mind, visions of the Powhantuwa people were joining the dance. She smiled. "Their spirits are at peace." She thought, "I must remember to tell Blue Cloud what I see..."

Little Bird's gentle sweet reverie came to a sudden halt when, in her mind, she saw another person's spirit joining the dance. She gasped, for the vision was the spirit of her grandson, Wamquwa. She looked over at him, and then at the face of Hoquia.

Hoquia looked sadly back at Little Bird and then lay her head down in the dirt. Little Bird knew by the pained expression on the face of Hoquia that she was experiencing a grim aura. They both arose and joined the praying circle. As she danced, Little Bird watched Wamquwa. He was looking northeast, toward the Big Waters, which lead to the Shanaquoix Village. His austere expression confirmed her fears. She knew he was in trouble.

Struggling to hold back her tears, she raised her hands to the sky and continued in the dance, praying even louder. She wanted to share her fears with Manakouk but waited until later. That night belonged to her love, Chief Blue Cloud.

After many hours, the tired group of people rested and slept. They rose early the next day to begin the trek home. Mid-journey, they stopped to rest and to share another meal. Then, the tribes parted and continued their own walk.

Little Bird was quiet as they traveled. It concerned Blue Cloud. He wondered if he had offended her. She spoke kindly to him, yet she seemed so sad. He could not keep his concern to himself. He slowed his horse and pulled the reins of hers to cause a slower gait. When they were both traveling at the same pace, he asked, "Little Bird, are you angry because we went to my village?" Little Bird answered a simple, "No."

Blue Cloud asked, "Then why are you so distant with me? We are best friends. We have shared many thoughts. Can you not tell me what is in your heart?" Little Bird answered, "Yes, I can, but not now, not here, not while we are with the others who can hear. Before we go to our sleep, I will tell you. It is not about you. I am happy for you. I felt your peace. I was also at peace." She silently added, "For a while."

Later that night, a tearful Little Bird related her vision to Blue Cloud. She told of the look on Hoquia's face. Blue Cloud did not minimize her fears, for he knew of her visions. All the Choptank people knew of the powers of Hoquia.

Blue Cloud could do nothing but hold Little Bird while she cried. After a long while, he said, "We must always pray for Wamquwa, that the spirits will keep him safe. The vision was a warning. You must tell him."

Little Bird was not sure about telling Wamquwa. She thought it better to confide in Manakouk first and ask his advice.

The next day, when the older couple approached Chief Manakouk, he was sitting on a log with his head down, dragging a twig, and drawing in the sand. He looked up. When Little Bird saw his mournful expression, she thought her vision had already come true. She asked him, "Where is Wamquwa?"

Manakouk replied, "He is not here. He left by the morning light. I saw him on his horse. He packed nothing for a journey. I ran after him. I tried to talk to him. I told him he was still sick from drinking too much. If he would just sleep, he would be better to think. He said he had much love for us, but he had to do something. I begged him to think of his family. He said he was no longer any good for them."

Manakouk continued, "I fear for him, but I also fear for our people. I feel he will try to reach the village of the Shanaquoix. They have declared peace with us.

If Wamquwa does something wild, he could cause harm to us."

Little Bird related her vision to Manakouk. Blue Cloud was remorseful that his own emotional closure was at the expense of his Choptank family. He knew the journey brought pain to Wamquwa. He sat helplessly on the ground and watched Little Bird weep.

Little Bird sensed what was in his heart. She tearfully said, "Blue Cloud, Wamquwa has been heading in this direction since the death of his father. He would eventually come to this day. You have no blame for any of this. You had a wonderful day of cleansing; please do not allow the poison of guilt to enter your spirit. Just be with me and pray for our grandson."

Love for Little Bird filled Blue Cloud's heart. Even in her time of grief, she worried about him and could still speak words of assurance. They spent the rest of the day by the Prayer Rock, praying to the Great Spirit on behalf of Wamquwa.

No one knew Manakouk had sent braves to follow him and let him ride out his hangover until the ride exhausted him; hoping he could ride out the anger. If that happened, they were to bring him back to the village to sleep but, he further instructed them to keep Wamquwa from causing harm to the tribe.

Wamquwa had no canoe, but Manakouk remembered seeing an abandoned one in the Powhantuwa village. He was sure he knew what Wamquwa was planning. The canoe, although too old and too small, was a part of his drunken plan.

The security of the entire tribe was at stake. Wamquwa had to be stopped.

The young braves, being led by Gray Wolf, a close friend of Wamquwa, followed Manakouk's instructions. They rode their horses a distance behind Wamquwa. One brave, in front, carried a white feather staff. As they traveled, they saw delegates of tribes guarding the peninsula.

The patrol recognized Wamquwa as a leader of the Choptank and let him pass. Wamquwa did not seem to know he was being followed but, the young men were sure that, even in his drunken stupor, he would eventually detect them. They continued to follow at a lengthy distance. He traveled the same path the tribe had just taken. He was riding hard, heading toward the village of the Powhantuwa. His obvious plan was to try a crossing of the Big Water and go to the Shanaquoix Village.

Gray Wolf contemplated sending a few men ahead to the village to hide the canoe but, he changed his mind. He wanted to give Wamquwa the dignity of making his own decision to forgo his futile attack on the Shanaquoix.

When Wamquwa rested, the young braves rested, taking turns at quick naps. They wondered if he would ever sleep. He was like a wildcat on a rampage, riding frantically and then lessening to an exasperatingly slow pace. They were sure he must have become aware of their presence and was drunkenly toying with them.

Gray Wolf knew his duty. He hoped his friend was sobering, would turn and head home. The chief's exact words were, "Prevent Wamquwa from reaching the village of the Shanaquoix."

The group knew they had to overcome Wamquwa, tie him to his horse, and return to the village with him. If he strongly resisted, and they could not constrain him, they would have to use extreme force. They hated the thought they might have to kill him to protect their people.

Wamquwa suddenly changed course, heading back toward the southern portion of the river. Wamquwa's head was pounding. He stopped at the bank of the river to wash his face and refresh his body for his continuing journey. Gray Wolf stayed as close to him as he dared. The braves, again, keeping a safe distance, followed. Suddenly, Wamquwa collapsed and fell asleep. The weary and relieved followers saw him lying spread eagle on the ground.

Gray Wolf sat nearby, allowing Wamquwa to sleep, and then to sober. The escorts took turns sleeping. It had been one full day. They had been trailing Wamquwa since before dawn. It was nearing sunset. They were all tired and wished to head back to the village, but Gray Wolf needed Wamquwa to be logical and willing to return to the village.

The young braves rested but created a perimeter to prevent Wamquwa from fleeing. Several hours later, he awoke. Suddenly remembering his treacherous plan, he was afraid he had somehow carried it out. He looked to the sky and screamed, "What have I done? What have I done? I killed him." He was afraid that he had offended the Shanaquoix, causing them to attack many villages. He thought, "They have already attacked my village. Oh, what have I done? What have I done?" He panicked, "My people! My people!"

Again, he repeated, "What have I done?" He vaguely remembered the canoe at the Powhantuwa Village. He remembered his plan to go back there alone and use it to go to the village of the Shanaquoix. Once there, he would cut off the head of their chief as he slept.

Wamquwa wondered if he had conducted his plan. He thought, "Yes, I must have, for I remember several braves behind me. They must be nearby. Why did they not kill me? Why am I alive? Are they toying with me before they kill me?" He wondered if he was even alive. He yelled, "Am I a spirit? Am I a spirit? I order you to tell me if I am a spirit."

The poor, hiding young braves were not sure how to react to Wamquwa's ranting. Gray Wolf was sitting with his face down. When he felt Wamquwa was coherent, he quietly said, "Wamquwa, I am your friend, Gray Wolf. Will you see my face?"

At the comforting voice of his friend, Wamquwa sobbed, "Yes. Yes. Please help me, Gray Wolf. I do not know where I am. I am almost blind. I cannot find my way back home. What horrible thing have I done?" He covered his burning eyes and continued to lament as Gray Wolf approached him.

Partly from exhaustion, partly from too much drink, but mostly from his grief-stricken memories and self-inflicted guilt of his father's horrible death, Wamquwa collapsed in the arms of Gray Wolf. He was a broken man. Gray Wolf assured him he had harmed no one, and that he was only following him as a friend, to keep him safe.

Wamquwa shook with relief. He attempted to get up but crumbled to his knees. Gray Wolf helped him to stand. As he did so, he signaled to the other braves to follow the plan, to stay out of sight and sound, but continue to follow at a safe distance. He lifted his weak friend to his own horse.

Wamquwa passed out. Gray Wolf secured him to the steed with a rope. They began their journey home. By not allowing Wamquwa to see the other braves, Gray Wolf hoped to spare him the knowledge and humiliation of other people being privy to his weakness. Under a moonlit sky,

Gray Wolf arrived at their village with Wamquwa unconscious and draped over his horse. The day was dawning. Manakouk sat watching as Gray Wolf untied Wamquwa's lifeless body. His heart was in excessive pain. He clenched his hands, creating fists. He quietly cried, "What have I done? What have I done?"

Suddenly, he saw Wamquwa move. He held back tears of relief when he realized his brother was alive, safely home and only sleeping off his drunkenness. He quickly sheltered his younger brother in the tent of Gray Wolf. Then, he sat close by, just outside, until the true morning light. The other braves went to sleep, vowing never to mention the incident. Little Bird wanted to go to Wamquwa, but Manakouk had forbidden anyone to see him until he was, hopefully, made well by the Healing Elder's medicine. Hoquia went in and out of the tent. Little Bird was a little resentful. She wanted to care for him. Manakouk reminded her that even Powhantuwa could not see him for that first day. Little Bird was happy her vision did not come true.

On the second day, they allowed Powhantuwa to see Wamquwa. It hurt her to see him so weak and humble. She held him as he wept. He cried, "My father is dead. Are the spirits angry with me? They will not let me forget the sack thrown at me. I almost did a horrible thing to you and our little Shaahatuck. I could have gotten you killed. In my mind, I thought I killed that chief. Gray Wolf told me I did not. Am I crazy, Powhantuwa? Am I crazy?"

Powhantuwa said, "No, you are grieving your father. If he had died from a sickness, you would grieve, but you would not hate. Now, you hate, but you cannot change what another person has done. Can you not pray to the Great Spirit? Have you ever?" Wamquwa answered, "No, my anger will not let me."

Even in his grief, Wamquwa felt better just talking with his beautiful Powhantuwa. After a while, he caressed her face and asked, "Could we please go to the nice place where we sleep?"

Powhantuwa, feeling secure enough to care for him, asked for and received permission from Manakouk to take Wamquwa to their tent. She did not realize the trial she had to endure. Nightmares plagued Wamquwa. He spent many nights wandering through the village. Many times, he overindulged in the fermented berry juices.

While trying to recover from the guilt of his father's death, Wamquwa was losing his own soul. His guilt was solely self-inflicted, but he battled mood swings so severe, Shaahatuck feared him. Manakouk posted a guard outside Powhantuwa's tent. Shaahatuck spent much of her time with her Aunt Hatsawa and Uncle Manakouk.

With Powhantuwa's love, Wamquwa dealt with his depression and regained his health. She continued to support him throughout the years. By the sixth year, he was close to being his old self, hunting, and fishing with his friends, playing with his family, praying to the Great Spirit, and playing games with the little six-year-old Shaahatuck. His soul was restored.

Powhantuwa was happy. Life was good again. That fact was obvious to her one day as she and Shaahatuck were picking berries. She realized she was humming and enjoying the constant chatter of her daughter.

Shaahatuck realized it. Looking over the bushes to her mother, she said, "Powhantuwa, you sound happy like Little Bird." Powhantuwa smiled as she thought, "Small Child. Big Emotions." She was both happy and saddened by those words from her daughter.

It was a sad fact that, for most of Shaahatuck's young existence, her father had never been a constant in her life. He was sometimes a lovable father, sometimes a playful friend, and at other times, an absolutely scary stranger. She had learned, even in her youthful innocence, to accept his love when offered, and then to hide from him and ignore his shortcomings when he was sad or drunk.

After a while, he became the peaceful, contented parent she needed, but he occasionally suffered depression.

The mother and daughter team finished picking berries. They walked back to the village with the other young women and girls. Wamquwa was waiting for them with a large smile on his face. He said to Powhantuwa, "I want to take you away for a journey." He said to Shaahatuck, "Hatsawa will watch you." It thrilled Shaahatuck. She would spend several nights with Tucahaunna and, especially, with Manassaquoit.

Even after six years and because of Wamquwa's mood swings, Powhantuwa feared to go on a journey alone with him. She felt safe near her protective brother-in-law, Chief Manakouk, but after much persuasion from Wamquwa, she took a chance, hoping the time away from the village would be beneficial.

As she rolled supplies in a blanket for their journey, she silently whispered, "Maybe life is getting better." She was more positive about the future.

CHAPTER NINETEEN
The Man with Gentle Eyes

Chief Manakouk and Blue Cloud enjoyed discussions during evening walks. Manakouk respected and revered Blue Cloud as a grandfather. He gleaned the older man's wisdom to solve tribal situations. Blue Cloud respected the strength of conviction with which young Manakouk led his tribe.

One evening, on such a walk, Blue Cloud, who had also grown to think of Manakouk and Wamquwa as his own grandsons, said to Manakouk, "I have been contented here with your people, Manakouk. You have learned the ways of peace." Manakouk said, "Blue Cloud, our people were not always peaceful people. My grandfather said our people were once angry wild people, fighting with other tribes for more land. One day, that all changed. My father loved to tell a story given to him by his grandfather's- grandfather, many, many moons ago." Manakouk related the story of his grandfather, Red Wolf, to Blue Cloud:

"Once, a man came to our people. They did not know from where he came. One day, he was just there, walking with them. They did not recognize his long garment. He had long hair and hair on his face. He was not of their people, but he knew them, and they knew him in their hearts.

"The Brave had gentle eyes. He spoke of love. He spoke of helping each other and praying to the Great Spirit. He walked with them for one sun and a moon. On the next Sun, he said he would leave our people with his peace.

The brave with the gentle eyes said to our people, 'Now, I must leave you, for I go to my Father in the clouds. "Someday, you will also be there with the Great Spirit, and you will be happy.' This made our people happy." Manakouk said to Blue Cloud, "That is why we say our dead go to the clouds to be with the Great Spirit,

We burn their bodies to cleanse their soul, so they are free to leave this home and go home to the Great Spirit. Their soul is sacred. We believe when our loved one lies on the burning bed, the smoke that rises from the flames is their spirit crossing our river to leave our world. Then, they go to the clouds to be with the Great Spirit. We pray He accepts the soul of the dead into His love, and we dance and chant to worship and please the spirits."

Manakouk continued, "This was not the custom of our people in the past." They buried their dead and then dug them up again after the flesh was gone from the bones. They kept them as sacred bones and took them when they moved their homes. We still follow the tradition of burying the bones and dig them and carry them if we move, but we do not move often. We are happy here. The spirits, especially the Great Spirit, blesses us."

Blue Cloud stopped walking as Manakouk finished his tale. He looked in amazement at Manakouk. He said, "I heard that same story from my father. I thought it was a good tale from the older braves. Gentle Eyes, yes, Gentle Eyes was the words my people spoke." Blue Cloud nodded in wonderment. He repeated, "Yes, those were the words of my grandfather, Gentle Eyes."

The two chiefs compared more of their story as they walked. Manakouk wished his grandfather, Red Wolf, had lived to tell stories to the grandchildren, but it satisfied him to have Blue Cloud teach them the ways of the Powhantuwa Tribe. He believed learning about the traditions of other tribes would instill respect for others in the hearts of tribal children.

CHAPTER TWENTY
The Plague

Shaahatuck was the joy of Wamquwa and Powhantuwa. They had no other children. Wamquwa once wondered if the Great Spirit had not given them more children because the spirits were angry with him for his evil thoughts. Over time, he dismissed the thought. He prayed often to the Great Spirit. He chanted the loudest when the tribe met for prayers. He no longer felt the guilt of his own father's death and was a good husband and father.

When Shaahatuck and Tucahaunna were eight years old, a sickness plagued the village. Hoquia and the Healing Elder gathered special herbs and made medicine packs to treat the infected members. Blue Cloud was one of the sickest. No herbs or broth would remove the harsh fever. Manakouk knew Little Bird was courting danger of becoming ill by caring for Blue Cloud. He knew her advanced age was against her, but he also knew his grandmother. She was a determined woman, and a devoted mate, so he let her do as she wished. Many tents in the Choptank Village held infected patients. No one had died from the fever, so Manakouk felt it would pass.

One evening, Powhantuwa came to tell Manakouk of Wamquwa's collapse. She did not stay to eat. She wanted to care for him. She promised to eat many good herbs, drink plenty of water, and to bathe in the river each day to cleanse her body of sickness. She needed to devote her time to the care of her mate. She asked Manakouk to give permission for Hatsawa to care for Shaahatuck. Manakouk stated, "This is not my wish, Powhantuwa. You will surely get sick. You should leave Wamquwa to the care of Hoquia and the Healing Elder. However, after encouragement from Hatsawa, he gave in to

Powhantuwa's plea; Powhantuwa re-entered her tent. The weary Healing Elder happily stepped out.

Manakouk walked through the village, looking into every tent. Out of the many homes, at least ten of them housed a sick member. He knew he had to do something. One sunrise, he took a morning meal to his grandmother's tent. Little Bird instructed, "Put it down, outside." She did not want him to enter her tent and become infected. Manakouk knew he had to stay strong for the tribe, so he obeyed his grandmother.

Blue Cloud sipped the broth Hatsawa had prepared. He smiled weakly at Little Bird. She ate no food, nor had anything to drink. She could not share her fears with anyone, but she knew Blue Cloud would soon take his journey across the river to the clouds. Blue Cloud collapsed and, in an instant, was asleep. Little Bird was weak but put up a pretense of feeling all right. When anyone called into her, she would answer, "Just tired. Only tired."

Once, while Blue Cloud slept, Little Bird went to Manakouk and Hatsawa. Keeping her distance, she reminded them she would not be joining the family for the evening meal. As much as he loved his grandmother, Manakouk wanted it that way because he did not want to tell her about Wamquwa's illness. He said to her, "Little Bird, I think you should not go near anyone until the sickness has passed." She gladly agreed. She was much too sick to be with anyone.

Hatsawa, covering her own mouth with one hand to avoid contamination, set a bowl of broth in front of Little Bird. For the same reason, Little Bird turned her head away. She sat a distance from them for a few minutes, sipping broth. She looked off at a distance where the children were engaged in games and meekly said, "My little ones. My little ones." When tears were threatening, Little Bird arose, took the broth, and walked back

116

to her tent. Hatsawa said, "Little Bird, it is only for a little while. Soon the sickness will be over. We will be a family again."

Little Bird sadly echoed, "Yes, only a little while." Suddenly, she turned and asked, "Where are Wamquwa and Powhantuwa?" Manakouk replied, "They're around somewhere." Little Bird nodded and continued her walk. After watching her stagger away, he asked, "Little Bird, are you sick?" Little Bird waved her hand in a farewell gesture, and replied,

"No, just tired," She repeated, "Just tired." She was sad that she could not see Wamquwa and Powhantuwa but was much too weak to be concerned for anyone except Blue Cloud. She entered the tent. Blue Cloud was moaning in his sleep. As she sat near him, memories of Moon Dancer and Running Doe, and many other members, now spirits, were in her mind.

Trying to rid herself of sad thoughts, Little Bird remembered happy times she and Blue Cloud shared while they were raising Powhantuwa. They had become her substitute parents early in her life. She gave them a second chance at parenthood. The birth of Shaahatuck created an even stronger bond between them and brought them immense joy. It was as if they had raised their own child.

Though Little Bird had not seen Powhantuwa or Wamquwa, the visit with Manakouk and Hatsawa, plus the chance viewing of her great-grandchildren, brought joy to her day.

Severe coughing interrupted Little Bird's joy and awakened Blue Cloud. He could barely speak. Little Bird gently said, "I will get you some water." Blue Cloud answered, "No. You will no longer care for me. You are too sick yourself. Little Bird, I have heard you moan when you think I am sleeping. I have felt your hot hands when you touch me. I hear you when you bring bad poison from your belly. I see you and my spirit is sad because I have done this thing to you." Little Bird asked, "How have you done this thing, Blue Cloud? How?"

Blue Cloud weakly whispered, "I do not want you to be as sick as me. I will soon cross the river and go to the clouds. Please do not touch me. Leave me to my sickness. Now you go away. I will soon be gone. Then the braves will take my body to the fire. I will be clean for you to care for my bones. You need to be strong, and you will be if you rest and eat."

Little Bird put her finger gently over the mouth of Blue Cloud and whispered, "The sickness is making you say words you do not mean." Cupping his face in her two hands, she said, "You must know you are my life. I will not let you cross the river without me." She attempted to caress his face with her own. Blue Cloud put up his weak hand to move her away. He whispered, "You will breathe my sickness." Little Bird whispered, "Yes." She gently put her lips to his face. They closed their eyes and fell asleep.

Late in the afternoon, Blue Cloud opened his eyes. Little Bird was barely breathing. With the little strength he had, he raised himself up into a sitting position. He called out, "Little Bird, come with me." Little Bird, thinking they were both spirits, had already crossed the river, and were on their journey to the clouds, asked, "How do you know where we go?"

Blue Cloud managed to smile. Crawling until he could pull himself up with his walking stick, he finally stood. He steadied himself, smiled at her again and said, "We are going to the river to see the sunset." Little Bird did not question him. She demanded one more mission from her old sick body. She stood and put her arm around his new thin frame. They walked out into the light and headed toward the river.

Hatsawa gasped when she saw the older couple struggling to walk. She started to run after them, to bring them back. Manakouk raised his hand and said, "No, do not stop them. They know what they are doing. My spirit sadly tells me what is in their heart." He smiled at her and said, "It will be the same for you and me when we are old." Hatsawa looked into the dark eyes she adored. She repeated his gentle words, "Yes, Manakouk, now, and when we are old."

Manakouk sent young braves throughout the village with a message to stay away from the river for a while, and that he would send another message when the ban was over. He sent another group to the river to summons everyone back to the village.

The old couple walked a short distance beyond the bend in the river, past the Prayer Rock, and to the river edge. When they were finally alone, Blue Cloud fell to the ground. He said, "Let me rest for a little while, then we will gather flowers." Little Bird silently questioned, "Flowers?" She asked herself again, "Flowers?" She thought his mind was leaving him, for he was speaking without logic.

After a few minutes, Blue Cloud, using his walking stick, pulled himself up to a standing position. Pointing to a bank full of yellow flowers, he asked, "Can you help me to the bank, there?" Little Bird was confused but nodded and indulged him. He picked flowers. Little Bird, although weak and confused, also picked flowers.

Their arms were full, but Blue Cloud kept picking. Their quest ended when Little Bird coughed and spit up blood. She dropped her flowers, fell over the bushes, and stumbled onto the sandy grasses. Blue Cloud put out his hand to support her. Her skin was hot to touch. He helped her to a sitting position. Little Bird cried when she looked into his near-death eyes. He smiled, touched her face, and continued picking the yellow flowers.

Little Bird staggered to the river's edge. After splashing her face, She dipped her skirt and filled it with water for Blue Cloud. As she turned to walk back to him, tears filled her eyes. Her frail mate was tossing flowers to make a circle. She smiled; knowing what he wanted to accomplish with the flowers, and how important it was for them to come to the beach. Her head was pounding. Her lungs could inhale only a little air, but her heart was full of love and joy. She dropped her water-filled skirt and struggled to walk back to him.

They needed no water.

Blue Cloud pointed to the water's edge. He smiled and said, "Look! Little Fox is dancing. She loves to dance." Realizing the meaning of the vision, Little Bird whispered, "Blue Cloud, do not leave me yet. Let me come to you." She stepped carefully into his newly created flower circle and reclined next to him, her head resting on his chest. Their bodies were feverish. The setting sun warmed their gentle souls. The sounds of the flowing river, with all its joyous accompaniments, were playing a love song. Its title was "Blue Cloud and Little Bird."

The elderly lovers lay quietly listening to the sounds of nature. Little Bird slowly looked up at Blue Cloud, and whispered, "I'm glad you came to our village." Blue Cloud embraced her even closer to his own body, enfolded her in his arms, and said, "I came to find you."

They held each other's weak hands, closed their eyes, and went to their eternal rest.

CHAPTER TWENTY-ONE
Cleansing and Renewal

The riverbank was a panorama of funeral fires. Powhantuwa came running out of her tent, screaming, "He is gone! He is gone!" The words would not take place in the head of Manakouk. His only brother was gone.

The fever had destroyed Wamquwa's disease weakened body and his young life was over. Just like that. It was over. Powhantuwa sobbed, "I failed him. I failed him. He is gone." Manakouk wanted to calm and reassure her, but his heart was with Wamquwa. He left her with Hatsawa and ran to the tent.

Hatsawa reminded Powhantuwa that the sickness was too strong even for the Medicine Man to heal; that she had done her best to care for her mate and should not grieve the spirits. Powhantuwa nodded her head in agreement and tried to stop crying.

When Manakouk saw his brother's lifeless body, he fell to his knees and sobbed. He stayed with Wamquwa for a while, so no one would see his grief. While he was there, he realized a terrible stench. He stepped out in the air and signaled for a few young braves to join him. He instructed them to prepare a burial bed, but to wait for a while to take the body. He wanted to give Powhantuwa a little time with Wamquwa before they took him to the burial fire. The stunned braves sadly did as he ordered.

Manakouk was sure he would need more burial beds, at least two more. He went to the tent of Little Bird and Blue Cloud. When he entered, the same rancid stench radiated from the hot animal skins. He realized that the inf was from the skins. He went to each tent where there was the sickness. Each time he entered, he put a cloth to his face to avoid the germs. They all had the same stench.

Manakouk took a young brave with him and walked to the edge of the village to check on his grandparents. He instructed the young brave to stand and wait for a signal before joining him.

He walked a short distance past the Prayer Rock. In a colorful 'Mating Circle' of yellow flowers, were the bodies of his grandparents. They were in a close embrace, holding hands. He called out to the young attendant, "They are dead. Tell Powhantuwa and Hatsawa to come to bless them."

To keep the contagion from entering his own body, Manakouk, again, covered his face with a cloth. He sat alone and wept for his grandparents. The splendor of the couple lying in death gave him a beautiful, bittersweet memory to cherish.

Powhantuwa was hysterical when told of her grandparent's deaths. They had been the only constant parents she had ever known. She could not bear to see them in death. She sent word to Manakouk that she would bless them at the fire. She needed to stay with Wamquwa for a few more minutes. That was all she could manage.

Manakouk understood. He and Hatsawa blessed the elder couple and said goodbye. He ordered the young attendant to get help and build burial beds. Three more members had succumbed to the sickness.

Chief Manakouk lit the first fire. Families lit the fires of their dead loved ones. The sight and odor of the burning beds sickened Manakouk. He remained silent for a while. Finally, he chanted and danced. As the flames consumed the bodies, everyone chanted, "Now you are cleansed by the fire. I pray to the Great Spirit to take you home. Now you are at peace."

Having those thoughts, and saying those words, reminded Manakouk of the stench in the tents where the sick people were dying. He realized that he had to, temporarily, keep the infected people and their caregivers away from healthy people.

After the funerals and the burying of the bones, Manakouk called an assembly. The members reluctantly gathered. Manakouk began, "There is still the sickness. We need to clean our village. Just as we cleanse our bodies when we go to the fire, we must use fire to stop the sickness."

These words struck a fearful note in the hearts of the members. They asked each other if he would burn every sick person. He raised his hand to stop the chatter. He said, "The sickness comes from the old tents. We must rid ourselves of them and make new ones. We have many new skins to create new homes. We cleaned them in the river. I will send you out of the village. You must wait for me to tell you when it is safe to return."

Manakouk spoke to his people about the healthy life his family enjoyed. He reasoned that it must be the daily ritual of bathing in the river. He said, "Our wonderful river has powers. You must bathe in its water more often." He then gave them his complete evacuation plan.

Whether they liked it or not, the tribe was divided, and they made their moves. The healthy male members took all the healthy members of the tribe to a separate location and set up a new temporary camp. They slept outside during the day, only entering the new tents at night.

The same healthy young braves moved the sick members to another location. They also slept outside but were covered with new blankets. Once they were out in the fresh air, they recovered.

The braves erected new dwellings, so the patients could rest peacefully in a cleaner environment. The remaining braves burned every tent and all articles of clothing belonging to the sick members.

Eventually, the village was clear of all signs of sickness. The sick members recovered. Manakouk allowed everyone to move their new tents back to the village.

For most of the Choptank Tribe, life was good again. For Powhantuwa, it was one of incessant depression. For the first year after the death of Wamquwa, she spent her days sleeping and walking the village perimeter at night. The members complained about her behavior.

Little Shaahatuck loved and wanted to be with her mother but was usually in the care of her Aunt Hatsawa.

CHAPTER TWENTY-TWO
Confession and Peace

Manakouk sat warming himself by the fire, thinking about the approaching cold season. He knew Wamquwa's death had been devastating for Powhantuwa. He had tried for several months to help her accept it and move on. She was so grief stricken that it was affecting the caregiving of her daughter.

Hatsawa had tried to be a good friend to Powhantuwa. She encouraged her to think of other braves as a new mate and a father for Shaahatuck. Powhantuwa could not even consider another mate. Her heart was still with Wamquwa.

One night, when Shaahatuck was asleep, Powhantuwa joined Manakouk by the evening fire. She sat quietly for a while, picked up a twig, poked it at the fire, and then tossed it into the middle of the flames. The blaze burst in response to the invasion of new fuel. Reacting to the eruption, she sharply caught her breath. Finally, she spoke, "Manakouk, I think I should leave your village."

A surprised Manakouk asked, "What? Why do you say that? Where would you go?" Powhantuwa nervously rubbed her hands together. She put them up to her mouth to keep from crying. Failing, she cried. Manakouk wanted to console her. He thought better. He needed to hear what she had to say. Obviously, she had this on her mind for a while and needed to get it out of her soul. He knew she needed to talk it through, so he listened.

Powhantuwa began, "I have been thinking of my life. The day Little Fox carried me to your village an evil spirit was chasing her. It killed her and entered me. Everyone who loves me suffers because of me. When I hear stories of your tribe, I only hear good stories. Once, when I was playing in the water with Little Bird, she laughed and told me how Running Doe squealed when Moon Dancer picked her up and whirled her around on the beach. I remembered my time with Moon Dancer and Running Doe. I have many memories of my young days, but I have more bad ones than good ones as I grew."

Powhantuwa related one memory to Manakouk:
"Sometimes, when Running Doe and I played in the water, Moon Dancer sat on the riverbank to watch us. He laughed when I fell, or when Running Doe slipped and fell into the water. Sometimes, the three of us played in the fields or in the water together, laughing and laughing.

Running Doe called the river, 'Powhantuwa's River.' She said my mother, Little Fox, blessed the river when she followed it to our village. Running Doe said when Moon Dancer showed me to her, she teased that the river washed me ashore to be their child. She said my mother was like a beautiful spirit who brought me to them.

Once when we were playing in the water. Moon Dancer sat watching us. I called him to come into the water, so did Running Doe. He did not look at her kindly, and he did not come into the water. She continued to play with me as if he did not matter. I felt sorry for him. He left us and went back to the village. Running Doe did not notice that he looked sad, but I did. Later, she also stopped laughing."

Powhantuwa continued, "I brought unhappiness to her and Moon Dancer. She no longer wanted me to be her daughter. Even before her death, Little Bird and Blue Cloud took care of me. I remember thinking my parents went off to be far from me because I brought them so much sadness."

Manakouk was shocked to hear such a story coming from Powhantuwa, whom he considered his sister. He told her, "Powhantuwa, Moon Dancer was chief of our tribe. He knew he needed to have a son who would be chief someday. He was angry because Running Doe never gave him that son. My father, White Horse, tried to force him to see the truth.

Speaking as a devoted brother, White Horse said to Moon Dancer, 'Maybe it is not her weakness.' Moon Dancer fought with my father for those words. He would not consider himself to have a blemish. He said Running Doe deceived him into becoming his mate; by telling him she would give him many sons. He grew to hate her for her treachery.

We all know Moon Dancer was wrong, but he and Running Doe fought because of their problems, not because of you. They loved you much. Their anger just grew too strong. They forgave each other. I believe they were lovingly together when the wolves attacked them."

Manakouk spoke with caution, for he was sure he knew the truth about Moon Dancer and Singing Bird. Many braves wanted her. She snubbed them all, always watching Moon Dancer. Running Doe never noticed.

After White Horse became chief, Manakouk asked him about the rumors. White Horse would only reply, "He wanted a son." It was that simple. Manakouk said nothing of this to Powhantuwa. When Hatsawa joined them, he asked Powhantuwa's permission to share her words. Powhantuwa agreed. She sat quietly by, playing with the ashes along the edge of the fire while Manakouk related her problem to Hatsawa. Hatsawa put her hand on the hand of Powhantuwa. She said, "Powhantuwa, we love you. You are our sister. You have brought no shame or evil spirit to our village. You have brought much joy." Powhantuwa cried out, "Wamquwa is dead because of me." Manakouk asked, "Why do you say that?"

Powhantuwa began, "When he grieved the death of your father, he was sick in his head. He did not seem to be the same person. The evil spirits would not let him sleep in peace. He had bad dreams. When he awoke, he was angry. He grew worse as time went on. When we were in the village of my people, an evil spirit must have taken control of him. Many times, I awoke with his hands around my throat. I thought he hated me. When he calmed, he was so sad. Sometimes, I loved him, sometimes I was afraid of him. Finally, after a long while, he seemed better. He was never the same Wamquwa, but he was better. He tried to be a loving mate. One day he said, 'Powhantuwa, I want to take you on a journey to show you the *Great Waters* on the far edge of our land.' I did not understand."

Powhantuwa said to Hatsawa, "Do you remember the time you kept Shaahatuck, so we could go away to be together?" Hatsawa nodded. Powhantuwa said, "We went to the *Great Waters*. The words of Wamquwa were true. It almost took the breath from my soul. I could not see any land except where we were standing. The sky was even bigger than here.

"My spirit swelled. I threw my hands up like wings. I wanted to run into the water and fly to the clouds, but Wamquwa held me back. He said the good spirits lived there in those waters, and we had to pray for permission to enter.

"He said he wanted to take me and Shaahatuck, and any other members who wanted to join us and build a new village there. He said we would pray to the spirits for permission to come into their waters. We would ask them to guide us as we prepare to settle there. We would make the 'Great Waters Area' our new home.

Atlantic Ocean

128

"He said he hated no one here, but he wanted a new life. I could not bear to hear it. I knew we were safe here with you. We do not know what tribes live there. They could be evil like the Shanaquoix and could have been watching us. I told that to Wamquwa, but when we returned, he made plans and spoke to others to join us."

Powhantuwa assured Manakouk, "No one agreed to go with him. They thought he still had a fever in his head, but he had plans for us to go. I prayed every sun and moon for him to change his mind. He did not.

When the sickness took him, I was so sad. If I had agreed to go with him, I think he would be alive. Then, the spirits gave him sickness, so he could not come to their Sacred Place, and we should not have gone there. I was praying against his prayers, and I caused his death. That is why I want to go away and leave your people at peace. My grandfather is gone now. There is no reason for me to stay."

Powhantuwa's story disturbed Manakouk and Hatsawa. For a while, they did not speak. Manakouk stoked the fire.

Finally, he spoke gently, "Powhantuwa, I have been to the Great Waters. Our Grandfather, Red Wolf, took Wamquwa and me there when we were young. It was as you say. I felt a strong presence of good spirits. Red Wolf said there was a peaceful tribe living near the Great Waters, but we saw no one. He said they always stay hidden when visitors come into view. He thought they were sacred guardians.

"Red Wolf told us that the waters were too strong for our canoes. We could never catch fish for our food. Children could not play on its edge because the sandy ground moves. He feared that it would carry them away. Therefore, we stayed in our village.' I remember it well.

"Our river is deep in some places but does not move toward us. It flows, so the water is always clean. It and our land have been good for us. The Great Spirit has blessed us with much food. We watch our children play and gather treasures on the edge of the river. It is our good home."

Manakouk reminded Hatsawa and Powhantuwa of the man with the gentle eyes who once came to their people. He blessed the people and the land and then went up to the clouds. Hatsawa nodded. Powhantuwa said she remembered her grandfather telling the story.

After a while of silent meditation, Manakouk sighed, and said, "Powhantuwa, you are not to blame for any of those bad times. I want you to remember how happy your grandfather and my grandmother were from the first time they met. They said many times. It comforted their hearts that your mother brought you to our village. I want you to remember that. They told me many, many times how you and Little Fox brought them together. They were gentle when they spoke. Theirs is a beautiful story. The Great Spirit blessed them in their old age. Yes, they had you to care for, because of the deaths of Moon Dancer and Running Doe, but you gave them a second chance to be parents and then grandparents in their later years. You were a beautiful part of their lives."

Powhantuwa stared blankly as Manakouk continued, "You have had many good walks. You brought joy to your people when you came out of the body of Little Fox. She, and her spirit guide, brought you to us. You had a good life here with Moon Dancer and Running Doe, and with your grandparents, for many seasons. When you became the mate of my brother, you created another wonderful life with him and gave us our beautiful Shaahatuck."

Manakouk repeated, "You had many good walks and many good dances, but now those walks, and those dances are over. You must make a new life for yourself and Shaahatuck."

Manakouk sighed and continued, "I will not tell you to mate, as others think I should. I want you to be happy for yourself. I want you to mate only when you are ready, or not to mate if you choose. I will always take care of you as my sister. I am not acting as your chief, only as your friend and brother."

The words of Manakouk brought peace to Powhantuwa. Tears welled in her eyes. She sat silently, hands in her lap. Finally, she smiled meekly and nodded. It was as if an enormous weight had been lifted from her shoulders. She sat staring at the fire, smiling as she thought of her parents and grandparents dancing with the spirits. It was a gentle smile. She felt such peace. No words could describe it. She said,

"Manakouk, I hope you live to be the chief of our tribe for many seasons. You are a good and kind chief. You know the words to teach, and to reach the heart." She stood and embraced both Manakouk and Hatsawa. She said, "I would like to stay by the fire for a little while."

Hatsawa also smiled. She had a loving affection and respect for the wisdom and compassion of her mate.

Manakouk nodded. He replied, "Someone will come by soon to tend the ashes." When he stood, a young brave approached the fire to tend it. Manakouk raised his hand and nodded his head toward Powhantuwa. The young brave understood. He stepped back to give her more time alone. Manakouk and Hatsawa left to go to sleep.

Manakouk nodded. He replied, "Someone will come by soon to tend the ashes." When he stood, a young brave approached the fire to tend it. Manakouk raised his hand and nodded his head toward Powhantuwa. The young brave understood. He stepped back to give her more time alone. Manakouk and Hatsawa left to go to sleep.

Powhantuwa sat watching the dancing flames. For the first time since Moon Dancer and Running Doe left her, she felt at peace with them. She thought about the wonderful love between her grandparents. Their death was a part of that love. She knew they were now happy with the Great Spirit. She wished she could have looked at their final flower circle, but she felt no condemnation. They had their love. She had hers. Recalling that sad day, she remembered that she needed to be with Wamquwa before he took his journey. She rose and walked to the edge of the village and looked at the river.

Even in the moonlight, she wanted to play in its waters. She smiled at that thought, lovingly remembering Moon Dancer and Running Doe. She regretted her selfish judgment. She remembered the comforting words of Manakouk and Hatsawa.

As she stood there, she realized how lucky she had been. Three mothers had blessed her: Little Fox, who bore her and died to save her life, Running Doe, who loved her as her own child, and Little Bird, who, even in the later part of life, adopted her and became a loving mate for the grandfather.

She prayed, "Great Spirit, you have blessed me for many suns and many moons. I am sorry for my bad thoughts. Please forgive me." She thought about the Metapoke Tribe and decided to ask Manakouk to take her to their village. She wanted to give gifts to them. She wanted to thank them for burying her tribal members, for rescuing her grandfather and caring for him. She especially wanted to thank them for bringing him to the Choptank Village.

Powhantuwa continued to thank the Great Spirit for leading the Metapoke guardsmen to Blue Cloud. She said special thanks to the Great Spirit letting him live, so he could tell her of her people. She prayed for the souls of her birth parents, Young Wolf, and Little Fox, and asked the Great Spirit to bless the Choptank people, for their nurturing, and for giving her the name, Powhantuwa. She remained standing, gazing at the river for a while, and then walked down the bank to the edge of the water.

There was a chill in the air, but Powhantuwa felt the warmth and love of the Great Spirit. The sand caressed her feet. The tolling of the water, as it beat against the rocks and logs jutting out into the water, sounded like a beautiful celebration. The resonating hum of nature was comforting to her soul. She finally felt the solace she had long been seeking. The wind blew at her long, blue-black hair, causing it to flow in the breeze.

The sand felt like a cushion beneath her feet. The mist from the river moistened her face. With both palms she waved moisture toward her; she caressed her cheeks. Then she smiled, cherishing the memories of many good times. She blessed the times yet to come, enjoying swimming and playing in the river she loved, and sharing her life with her beautiful daughter, Shaahatuck.

She closed her eyes for a moment, allowing the memories of a happy Moon Dancer and a beautiful Running Doe to appear. Then, she remembered a sweet older couple holding hands as they walked up the beach and stepped into the middle of their flower circle. She whispered a promise to be a better mother to Shaahatuck.

Finally, she visualized Wamquwa, as he grabbed her hand and led her into the forest. She smiled at their 'wonderfully wicked' lovemaking before their mating. She remembered the evening of their mating.

Remembering Wamquwa's large hand resting on her shoulder as they danced, she sighed, "That was a good day, Wamquwa! Ours was a 'Good Day.' We had a 'Good Walk.' We had a 'Good Dance.' Now our dance is over. I want you to be happy in your new life. I will be happy in mine. Life will be good for our little Shaahatuck." She knelt, cupped her hands together, scooped up water, arose, and let the water flow over her fingers, symbolically releasing her hold on the spirit of Wamquwa.

Saying her farewell, Powhantuwa took off her mating beads, gently tossed them into the river, watched as they flowed with the moving water and whispered, "Wamquwa, thank you for sharing your river and your life with me." Then, she raised her hands and spoke to the river. "Maybe you brought me here." Taking a deep spirit-filled thankful breath, she added, "If you did, I am happy it is so."

She smiled peacefully, remembering Running Doe's words, describing their area of their beautiful river as, 'Powhantuwa's River.' She knew generations to follow would continue to call it the 'Mighty Choptank,' for it was. But, for that day, it pleased her to think of it as her deliverer, her own river. She lovingly whispered, "You were right, Running Doe. It is home.

It is 'My Home.' A wonderful, wonderful home.

To me, and for this day… it is

"Powhantuwa's River.

Remember,

There is love all around us. We just need to look

"For The Love"

www.ingramcontent.com/pod-product-compliance
Lightning Source LLC
Chambersburg PA
CBHW071350170626
46811CB00003B/1064